P9-DXC-749

AMBUSH ALLEY

The alley was filled with broken bottles and soggy, rotting paper and broken crates. But Raider could see a man hunkered down behind a discarded barrel.

Raider started to lift a hand, intending to hail the fellow.

His gut wrenched as he realized the man behind the barrel was holding a shotgun. And the scattergun was pointing square at Raider's chest. Raider threw himself backward into the loose, rotten trash inside the alley mouth just as the shotgun roared.

Raider shifted to his left in a squirming roll, and the scattergun bellowed again. . . .

Other books in the *RAIDER* series by
J. D. HARDIN

RAIDER
SIXGUN CIRCUS
THE YUMA ROUNDUP
THE GUNS OF EL DORADO
THIRST FOR VENGEANCE
DEATH'S DEAL
VENGEANCE RIDE
CHEYENNE FRAUD
THE GULF PIRATES
TIMBER WAR
SILVER CITY AMBUSH
THE NORTHWEST RAILROAD WAR
THE MADMAN'S BLADE
WOLF CREEK FEUD
BAJA DIABLO
STAGECOACH RANSOM
RIVERBOAT GOLD
WILDERNESS MANHUNT
SINS OF THE GUNSLINGER
BLACK HILLS TRACKDOWN
GUNFIGHTER'S SHOWDOWN
THE ANDERSON VALLEY SHOOT-OUT
BADLANDS PATROL
THE YELLOWSTONE THIEVES
THE ARKANSAS HELLRIDER
BORDER WAR
THE EAST TEXAS DECEPTION

RAIDER

DEADLY AVENGERS

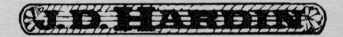

J.D. HARDIN

B

BERKLEY BOOKS, NEW YORK

DEADLY AVENGERS

A Berkley Book/published by arrangement with
the author

PRINTING HISTORY
Berkley edition/October 1989

All rights reserved.
Copyright © 1989 by The Berkley Publishing Group.
This book may not be reproduced in whole or in part,
by mimeograph or any other means, without permission.
For information address: The Berkley Publishing Group,
200 Madison Avenue, New York, New York 10016.

ISBN: 0-425-11786-3

A BERKLEY BOOK® TM 757,375
Berkley Books are published by The Berkley Publishing Group,
200 Madison Avenue, New York, New York 10016.
The name ''BERKLEY'' and the ''B'' logo
are trademarks belonging to Berkley Publishing Corporation.

PRINTED IN THE UNITED STATES OF AMERICA

10 9 8 7 6 5 4 3 2 1

CHAPTER ONE

Raider came floating up from sleep slowly and gently. Eyes still closed and senses suspended somewhere between dream and wakefulness, he was dimly aware that he felt like he was drifting on warm, languid waters. Like he was floating in a tub of heated water. Like somehow he had fallen asleep in the bath and the bath water remained miraculously hot the whole night through, which was of course ridiculous but nevertheless was the feeling he had at this moment of half sleep. He kept his eyes closed tightly, and gave himself over to the sensations. He was conscious enough now to realize that the dreamlike feelings were pleasant ones. He was surrounded by warmth, by moisture. In particular, his pecker was surrounded by warmth and moisture. His morning erection was firm and insistent, the demands of it drawing him closer and closer to full consciousness although he resisted that pull and tried to hang onto the pleasures of a deep, lazy sleep.

It was still dark out. He could tell that without opening his eyes. And he did not want to wake up. Not yet. Not for quite a while. Particularly since he was so thoroughly enjoying this dream. The dream was so good—and last night had been so long and so late—that he did not want to give up sleep quite yet.

The dream sensations continued warm and wet. En-

1

gulfing. Suspending. Floating gently like a tide. Rising
and falling. Up and down. Slow and easy. He smiled a
little and stretched, pushing his hips forward in search
of more of that slow, dreamy pleasure. He felt a tight-
ening of the warm ring that enveloped his cock, then a
sudden withdrawal. There was a sound of gagging and
a muffled cough, then the sensations returned

Raider snapped fully awake, his eyes coming open to
the half-light that filled the hotel room. He wasn't
asleep now, by damn, yet the sensations continued.

He peered around. He seemed to be alone in the
lumpy bed, the pillow beside him empty of the blonde
hair that had been there last night. But there was a
bulge under the sheet at his right side. And those
maddeningly delightful sensations kept right on.

"Hey!" He flipped the sheet back.

Marta turned to look at him. She had an impish
twinkle in her eyes. A cat-that-caught-the-canary grin.
Except it was no canary, or any other feathered thing,
that was trapped between her rosy lips. Raider thought
she looked cute as hell like that.

She released him and sat up, brushing her hair back.
The gesture emphasized the swell of her breasts, which
were large and soft and blue-veined beneath their pale
surface.

"Did I wake you? Sorry." A lie, of course. She
didn't sound the least bit sorry. Nor, frankly, was
Raider.

He reached for her, pulling her up beside him again.
"Sorry, eh?"

She shrugged and giggled.

He pulled her to him, flattening her breasts against
his chest. Marta slipped her arms around him and hooked
a leg over his waist. She kissed him, then dipped her
head lower and began to run the tip of her tongue over
his chin and across his throat. She was making small,
impatient sounds low in her throat.

Raider gave in to her insistent tugging, rolling on top

of her. Then into her. She opened herself to him and once he was socketed deep inside her wrapped herself leechlike around him, clinging to him with arms and legs and mouth as if wanting to consume him and take all of him totally inside her pliant body.

Marta was a big girl. Big tits, wide hips, pale eyes. She had a mane of thick, untamable blonde hair and an honest approach to her own physical appetites. She liked to fuck, which she had told him point-blank within five minutes of their meeting yesterday afternoon. Someday she would find a nice, sensible Polish man to marry her and care for her and provide the babies she knew she would want then. But that wouldn't happen for several years yet. Not until she was well into her twenties. In the meantime—

She laughed happily and pulled him deeper into her, her back arching off the soft mattress to meet his thrusts, her fingers raking his back and urging him on.

Raider responded eagerly. Driving. Pumping. He did not have to slow down at all to let Marta catch up. Hell, she was ahead of him to begin with. He was having to catch up with her.

Their bellies slapped together with loud, moist plopping sounds that came quicker and quicker as the pace intensified. Marta's head lolled back and her lips drew tight against her teeth. Cords of taut sinew stood out on the side of her neck as her body tightened like a bowstring beneath Raider's hammering hips. She stiffened and clenched, ripples of shuddering force sweeping through her as she reached satisfaction.

Raider continued to slam deep into her, riding hard and fast now, until his balls exploded and emptied in a convulsive flow. He held himself poised over her for a moment, then collapsed onto her warm, sweaty body.

Marta sighed, kissed the side of his neck briefly and then shoved at his chest, already trying to wriggle out from beneath him.

''What's this, no seconds? How come you're in such

a hurry?'' Raider was spent but already thinking about
another round.

Marta shook her head. "Gotta go, dearie. That's why
I woke you so early. I'm a workin' girl, you know. I
don't wanta be late.''

Raider grunted and sat on the side of the bed rubbing
his eyes. "Cain't say that I'm complainin'. You know
how t' wake a fella just fine.''

Marta grinned and reached for the black cotton stock-
ings she had discarded the night before.

"What the hell time is it, anyhow?''

She squinted toward the window blinds, just now
beginning to show a pale gray around the edges. "Six?
I dunno.''

He groaned.

Still, he was awake now, and if Marta was leaving he
might as well get up too. Lazing abed of a morning was
just fine for two but not amusing for someone alone.
Raider stood and stretched. Behind him Marta gave an
appreciative whistle and a wink. What she saw seemed
ordinary enough to him, but women tended to like what
they saw when they looked at him. He wasn't complaining.

Raider was tall, well over six feet, with wide shoulders and a horseman's narrow hips. He had black hair,
in need of trimming at the moment, and a sweeping
black mustache that he preferred to tend himself. His
face was craggy and weathered, his body marred here
and there with the scars and abrasions of a life somewhat rougher than most.

He stretched again, belched, and reached for his
clothing. He had to take a leak and wash off the sticky
remains of several encounters with Marta, but the wash-
room was down at the end of the hall. He pulled on
worn jeans, a checked flannel shirt, and a pair of tall,
stovepipe boots, then seated a gunbelt around his hips
before picking up a worn leather jacket and black,
low-crowned Stetson.

"Will you be around t'night, dearie?'' Marta asked.

She made no attempt to hide the hopeful note in her voice.

"More'n likely," Raider answered. "There ain't a damn thing goin' on lately t' take me anyplace interestin'." Chicago, in his opinion, was not all that interesting. Marta, on the other hand, was.

"I'll look for you at the café," Marta volunteered. "Same place we met. I'll be there by seven." She winked again. "I'll wait if I have to." She finished buttoning her shirtwaist, fluffed her hair without bothering to try to pin it without a mirror and brush and came around to his side of the bed so she could rise on tiptoes—even though she was tall enough that she likely found that rarely necessary—and kiss him good-bye.

"I'll prob'ly be around," he said, not exactly promising that he would be.

"I have some fun things in mind we can try if you make it, dearie," Marta suggested.

Raider gave her a slap on the rump and saw her out the door. He yawned again, then picked up his shaving gear and the dingy towel provided by the hotel management and headed down the hall.

It was so early, he realized, that even if he dawdled over breakfast he was going to be damned early reaching the office.

The big man grinned quietly to himself. Now wouldn't that shake the hell out of Allan Pinkerton? It was as good as unheard of that Raider would show up early for work. And to think it was going to be wasted on a dry spell when there wasn't shit for interesting cases going on at the Pinkerton Detective Agency. If nothing else, he decided, maybe his early arrival would give the boys at the office something to gawk and gossip about for the rest of the day. Better that than nothing at all. Sure would be nice, though, if something came up today. Raider was getting tired of sitting around in Chicago waiting for an assignment.

CHAPTER TWO

"Missin' person? You want *me* t' go out on a penny ante missin' person case? Bullshit!"

"That's right," Allan Pinkerton growled.

Raider continued to pace and prowl the threadbare rug in front of Pinkerton's desk. "I cain't b'lieve this crap," he complained. "You want me t' go out on a stinkin' missin' person thing. Damn it, don't you have a train robbery someplace? A bank holdup? What the hell's the matter with all the crooks out there? They all on fuckin' vacation or somethin'?"

"Look Raider." This time it came out with more of a bellow than a growl. "I won't have you turn into a prima donna. I've been paying you to sit and do nothing these past few days, and of course I want you to take this case. You're the best man I have here, and it's time you earned your keep."

Raider stopped his pacing but refused to sit. He felt insulted by the suggestion that the Pinkerton Detective Agency's best operative should be asked to undertake a measly missing persons case. He had been saying so in no uncertain terms for the better part of five minutes now.

"Fer cryin' out loud; any asshole with a mail order detective's tin can take on missin' persons. Give the case t'—hell, I dunno—give it to an office boy. Give it

6

t' somebody what needs some experience. Surely you don't mean t' send me off on a dipshit thing like this! It's belittlin', that's what it is." He paused and blinked. Belittling. Good word. He was proud that he'd thought of it in the heat of the moment.

"I have no other cases to give you, damn it, and I won't have you hanging around gambling and whoring on my time," Pinkerton declared.

Raider glared across the desk at the aging head of the agency that bore his name.

The son of a bitch, Raider swore, was the very model for every penny-pinching-Scotsman joke that ever was. Allan Pinkerton was a Scot and he was a penny-pincher with a vengeance. The man couldn't abide the thought of an employee with free time on his hands. It was driving him wild that his number one operative was sitting around Chicago drawing pay instead of being out somewhere generating income for the firm.

This state of affairs had been going on for the better part of a week now, and neither Raider nor Allan Pinkerton was happy with it. Raider was bored—with certain interruptions like Marta Pobreski providing exception to that rule—and Allan was frantic to find work for him.

"Besides," Pinkerton went on, "the gentleman in Omaha is entitled to my very best man on this case. He's willing to pay a bonus to the firm for finding his sister."

Raider groaned. If there was anything Pinkerton could not resist it was a freely offered bonus over and above the agency's normal rates.

But a missing persons case?

"You'll pack your gear and you'll go nice and polite to Omaha and find the gentleman's sister for him and you'll earn your keep for a change," Pinkerton asserted.

"You don't even know anythin' about this case," Raider complained. He had seen the wire from Roy Sigmond requesting that the agency find his missing sister.

"I don't have to be the one to know," Pinkerton countered. "That's what operatives are for. You can tell me about it in your reports."

Raider made a face.

"Do you want the case or must I lay you off on non-paid vacation?" Pinkerton challenged.

"Non-paid?"

"That's what I said."

Raider growled at his boss, but he was stuck with this one, and he knew it. He happened to be broke at the moment, thanks to a run of bad luck with the cards this past week while waiting for a case to break. But damn it all anyway. A lousy missing persons case!

"Which will it be?" Pinkerton persisted.

"Omaha," Raider snapped.

Pinkerton gave Raider a smile of victory and laced his hands over his paunch, leaning back in his chair.

Now that Raider had given in, Pinkerton seemed perfectly satisfied.

"You know where to find Mr. Sigmond?"

"Yeah," Raider grumpily admitted. The telegraph message told them that.

"Frequent reports, Raider. Don't forget." The battle with his top operative now over, Pinkerton turned his attention to a file spread open on his desk.

Raider hesitated only a moment, then let himself out.

Omaha was all right, damn it, but a missing persons case? He grumbled the whole way back to his hotel and off to the rail depot. He was still silently bitching when he reached Omaha.

CHAPTER THREE

Roy Sigmond greeted him with enthusiasm, grabbing Raider's offered hand in both of his and pumping it up and down with obvious relief. "Thank you, thank you for coming." He said it over and over, even after Raider disengaged himself from the clinging handshake and stood awkwardly in the doorway of the client's hotel suite.

After a bit Sigmond seemed to realize the discomfort he was causing. He gave the big man a look of sheepish apology and motioned the Pinkerton operative inside. "Sit over there. Please." He guided Raider toward an armchair and a small side table already set with cigars, a humidor of tobacco, glasses, and decanters of wines, liquors, and liqueurs to satisfy damn near any taste. Raider gathered that Roy Sigmond wasn't a man who had to do things on a tight budget. The cost of a single night in a suite like this would keep a working-class family for a long time. But Raider hadn't come here to be impressed with Roy Sigmond or the man's riches.

"Can we git down to it?"

"Certainly, yes, absolutely." Sigmond was smiling. And despite the words of agreement he blithely ignored the request and went instead to tap on a closed door leading to another room of the luxurious suite. "Our guest has arrived, dear. The Pinkerton detective?"

A moment later the door was opened and a tall, stunningly beautiful woman came into the sitting room to join the gentlemen.

"My dear, this is Mr. Raider from the detective agency. Mr. Raider, my wife, Eleanor."

Raider wasn't all that much impressed by Sigmond's show of wealth. But he was damned well impressed by Mrs. Eleanor Sigmond.

The woman must've been nearly six feet tall, and she was built like a race horse. And a fine-blooded one at that. Sleek and shiny and bred for speed.

Her hair was the color he's heard called platinum, which was a blonde so pale it looked white. Except on Eleanor Sigmond there wasn't anything about the color that made her look old. Her husband Roy was likely in his late forties or early fifties, but the little lady—little? she damn near looked Raider square in the eye when she stood in front of him with her hand extended— couldn't be more than in her very early twenties. Her complexion was pale and perfect. She wore a silvery gray gown that matched perfectly her pale gray eyes. And she carried herself like she knew exactly how good she looked and was damn well proud of it. Just a hair short of being smug.

Raider stood to accept the introduction—he still had all the bark on, but he'd learned a few things too—and when she extended the tips of her fingers for him to touch he remembered how to make a leg and bow over the fingertips without actually slobbering on the back of the elegant woman's hand.

When he straightened and looked into Mrs. Sigmond's eyes Raider's heart thumped in his chest as if it wanted to escape. The woman didn't say or do anything to make him feel that way. It was just something about her. An air of raw, serious sensuality surrounded Eleanor Sigmond, just floated in the atmosphere about her, like cheap perfume on a four-bit whore. This was a woman who could make men bark at the moon with the slightest crook of her finger.

Raider looked her in the eyes and did his damndest to ignore all of that. "Pleasure, ma'am."

"And mine, sir." She inclined her head slightly and smiled. The sight of her smile made Raider's toes curl.

A couple of feet away Roy Sigmond was beaming with the pride of ownership. He was showing off, and they all knew it. Hell, Raider couldn't blame him. Eleanor was a prime example and worth some crowing over.

"Will you do the honors, my dear?"

Eleanor inclined her pretty head graciously once again. "Your preference, sir?" She motioned toward the table of drinks. Her voice was throaty. Somehow it reminded Raider of the smoky, peaty flavor of some very old, very fine Scotch whiskey he'd once tasted.

"Whiskey. Neat."

Again that cool, seductive nod, and she drifted over the floor to pour whiskey for Raider and small glasses of pale wine for her husband and herself.

Raider flopped back into the armchair, feeling like a country bumpkin plunked unwillingly into a palace.

Roy Sigmond watched and beamed throughout all of this, obviously enjoying Raider's reaction to Eleanor and just as obviously relishing the sight of his discomfort. Not in any nasty way, though. More like it was a reflection of Sigmond's own exceptional taste and good fortune.

Sigmond waited until they were all served and seated, Eleanor perched on the forward few inches of a delicate antique chair with her back straight as a drill sergeant's, before he got around to the business that had brought Raider here.

"Yes." He harrumphed and coughed into his fist. "You mentioned something about business, I believe?"

"Reckon I did," Raider drawled. He took a swallow

of the whiskey. The stuff was smooth as mountain spring water and spread warm and easy in his stomach.

"I presume you read my telegram?" Sigmond asked.

"Yeah. It don't say all that much, though." Eleanor, he noticed, was silent but attentive.

"In short—" Sigmond began.

"Short ain't what I need t' hear," Raider interrupted. "If you want me t' find somebody, I expect we'd best have the long version on th' table."

Sigmond nodded and paused to take a sip of his wine. As far as Raider could tell Eleanor was interested only in holding the stem of her glass. She hadn't touched any of the wine yet.

"Very well," Sigmond said.

He commenced to talk, and the three of them sat in the room there for the better part of an hour until Raider had about all of it that he could expect to get. Eleanor rose periodically to freshen the men's drinks but never did get around to tasting any of her own.

Roy Sigmond and his sister Violet grew up in northeast Utah. Later on Violet left the family home, in mining country in the Uinta Mountains, and moved to Salt Lake City. Fled home rather than moved away from it, Sigmond admitted reluctantly. Something had happened between Violet and their father. They'd argued violently, and Violet had run away in the middle of the night. The subject of Violet's departure wasn't ever discussed in the family afterward, so Roy really didn't know all that much about it.

What he did know was that Curtis Sigmond was dead now, and Roy was the owner of one hell of a lot of productive mining property. Roy was the owner, that is, *and* Violet. She was entitled to half the wealth, and Roy figured to see that she had it. Which was where Raider and the Pinkerton Detective Agency came in.

Roy didn't know where Violet had gone since she'd run away from home.

He knew she'd gone to Salt Lake immediately after she left Silver Canyon. A friend had seen her there. Spoke to her there. She'd pretended not to know him. This friend thought, from something he'd overheard, that Violet had changed her name when she was in Salt Lake and was now calling herself Violet Thorn.

"That was probably something of a quiet joke," Sigmond speculated. "Violet always did like to play on words, so I would presume that she was playing on her own name when she chose that name. She truly isn't a thorny person, though. Anything but. But she must have had some thorny problems to face when she went out on her own, with no support or goal save escape."

She was no longer in Salt Lake City. Sigmond was sure of that. He would have been able to find her there, but she seemed to have disappeared completely.

Violet left home late the previous summer, about nine months ago. Sigmond hadn't seen or heard from her since. Now that their father was dead he wanted to find her and bring her back to her inheritance.

"I can't imagine the conditions she may be living under, Mr. Raider. She had nothing when she left Silver Canyon. Nothing. And there is so much—" He motioned vaguely around the sumptuously appointed hotel suite. "Please find her for me, Mr. Raider."

"What if she don't wanta come back?"

Sigmond frowned. "I'm sorry. I haven't made myself clear, have I? I do not want the Pinkerton Agency— you that is—to bring her home. I merely want you to locate her for me.

"Simply tell me where I can find her, Mr. Raider. Violet has always been shy with strangers. If you were to approach her it could frighten her dreadfully. Certainly it would worry her.

"No, what I want you to do, Mr. Raider, is to discover for me Violet's whereabouts. Then I shall go to her at once, explain the changed circumstances at home and lead her back to the bosom of her family."

He smiled and spread his hands happily, as if the act of explanation made the request as good as accomplished.

"Sounds kinda simple," Raider said. He finished the whiskey in his glass. Immediately Eleanor moved to refill it.

Lordy, but she was one sexy woman. When she steadied Raider's glass her fingers touched the side of his hand. He could feel the heat from her. It was like her flesh was charged from some kind of storage battery, except the charge given off wasn't electricity but pure sexual energy.

"Please do find dear Violet, Mr. Raider," Eleanor said in that husky, seductive voice. "Please bring her home to us." Eleanor smiled, and it was like she'd gone and turned up the wicks on the lamps in the room. Raider found himself wanting to rush out and grab Violet Sigmond by the ears and drag her home. Just to get another smile from Eleanor.

"Yes, ma'am," he heard himself saying. "I'll sure try an' do that for you."

Across the room Roy Sigmond beamed and laced his hands over his stomach as he leaned back in his chair. "Naturally," he said, "I shall expect progress reports from you frequently. Preferably on a daily basis."

Raider frowned. He didn't like reports and paperwork anyway. And daily?

"I shall want to be immediately available to rush to Violet's side when she is located, Mr. Raider, so I shall follow close behind you during the course of your, um, investigation. I shall make sure you know where to reach me at all times. And I shall expect the same courtesy from you." He smiled again. "Naturally I shall pay a handsome bonus in exchange for this service. To the Pinkerton Agency and, ahem, an additional bonus to you personally." His smile became wider. "I don't want dear Violet remaining in her state of exile a single moment longer than is necessary, sir. I trust you appreciate my concern and will cooperate."

"I ain't much for reports," Raider told him quite honestly. "But I'll do my best, I reckon."

"I am sure that will be more than adequate, sir." Sigmond beamed. Eleanor smiled.

Later, when Raider excused himself and went down a floor to the room Sigmond had reserved for him in Omaha's most expensive hotel, he was thinking that just for one night he would damn sure like to swap places with Roy Sigmond. He wouldn't mind crawling between the sheets with a hot-blooded handful like Eleanor Sigmond. That one was about enough to set a man afire.

CHAPTER FOUR

This was damn sure a new experience. Before Sigmond and Eleanor saw Raider off the next morning, Roy handed him a sheaf of fifty-dollar bills thick enough to gag a goat.

"Expense money," he explained with a smile. "When you work for me, Mr. Raider, I expect you to travel in style and comfort. Spare yourself nothing. And, ha ha, I expect no close accounting afterward. If you take my meaning. First class, man. The very best. That's what I believe in; that's what I give, and that's what I expect in return. The very best, eh?" The man was as good as saying he wouldn't care if some of the cash stuck to Raider's fingers. And the expense money was over and above the agency's fees.

There was—Raider had to stop and count it when he was comfortably settled in a private luxury compartment on the Union Pacific running west from Omaha—two thousand dollars right there in his hand. And Sigmond had told him that if he wanted more all he had to do was mention it.

"I have business to attend to here before I can follow," Sigmond had also said, "but I shall be along behind you shortly. You can reach me at the hotel here until tomorrow morning, then at the Grand Simeon in Salt Lake City."

16

Raider had never heard of a place in Salt Lake called the Grand Simeon. But then it was likely the kind of place that would be out of his reach.

Sure as hell was nice to be traveling at the upper edge of first class, though, he discovered. There was a waiter in the car who seemed to do nothing but lurk in the hallway outside Raider's door just waiting for Raider to want something so he could jump to fetch it.

And come nightfall there was no fretting about getting a stiff neck from trying to catch a bit of sleep while propped into the corner of some grimy coach seat. Instead the waiter out in the hall—called, Raider learned, a valet—came in and fixed out a bed with sheets and fluffy pillows and even turned the sheets down so Raider wouldn't have to do such manual labor for himself, then laid out a peppermint candy and a cigar in case one of them would please.

Raider arrived in Salt Lake feeling like a robber baron. All he needed now was a gold-headed cane and a silk top hat to make it all complete. Though he thought those might go kind of strange with his tattered jeans and disreputable leather jacket.

CHAPTER FIVE

Often the quickest way to get something done is also the simplest. Bright and early the next morning Raider headed for City Hall.

Salt Lake was a nicely laid out city, with wide streets, fine buildings, and everything planned and managed to the smallest detail. This was no overgrown boom camp with the streets ambling wherever the cow paths used to be, but a solid community that somebody had carefully designed before they began building it.

If they paid that much attention to the layout of the streets, Raider figured, maybe they would pay attention to who lived on those streets too.

The folks in charge were friendly, courteous, and helpful. The clerk behind the counter Raider went to was in his early twenties, quick with a nod and a smile and actually eager to be of assistance.

"Miss Violet Sigmond, you say?"

"That's right, Mister—?"

"Waters," the clerk told him cheerfully. "Harvey Waters. One moment please, sir. I'll see what I can find."

Waters hurried away and returned moments later with a huge, bound record book and a somewhat smaller book perched on top of it. He pushed the small book toward Raider and said, "I'll look through the tax

18

records. You're welcome to see them yourself, of course, but it will be quicker if I do it. Meanwhile why don't you look through here." The book he gave Raider turned out to be a city directory.

There was no listing for a Violet Sigmond in the directory. Nor, Waters said, was there anything in the tax records under that name.

"Let's try Violet Thorn," Raider suggested. "I, uh, understand that might've been her married name." That part, of course, was made up, but it was a convenient explanation for why a woman's name would change. He did not want to have to go into details with Harvey Waters about why a young woman would want to change her moniker.

Waters bent to the tax records again while Raider sifted through the directory a second time. Again there was no mention of a Violet Thorn in the small book.

"This could be something," Waters suggested. He turned the big tax book and pointed to a listing written in a fine, spidery hand.

Raider grunted.

The listing Waters showed him referred not to Violet Thorn but someone named Lester A. Thorn.

"I don't think so," Raider said.

"If you say so," Waters told him doubtfully. "But I should mention that we rarely show a woman as a head of household or a property owner. Our records normally would relate to the, um, gentleman of the household, not to the wife, if you see what I mean."

"Sure." Raider was trapped in his own small lie now that he'd voiced it. He couldn't go back and explain that Thorn was an alias used by a girl hiding out from her father.

"Let me see now." Waters helpfully turned the book back around, kept a finger at the indicated listing, and flipped forward to a cross-reference something. "Yes. Here we have it. Lester A. Thorn. A carpenter. Doing business at The Gates. Home listed at the same address.

That would be, um, along the canal, if I remember correctly. South of here and a few blocks west." He smiled. "Just ask anyone. They'll help you find it. We have a very logical street numbering system. Almost impossible to get lost here."

Raider thanked the helpful clerk but cussed himself for not thinking out the fib beforehand.

"If there is anything more I can do for you, anything at all—"

"I'll surely let you know," Raider told him.

Waters collected his record books and disappeared into the stacks of shelving behind the counter.

Raider ambled out into the bright, mid-morning sunlight and went to find a café where he could have some coffee and do some thinking. He ordered coffee and a doughnut. They were promptly brought by a plump, red-faced waitress.

While he chewed the gooey sweet, Raider pondered his next step.

Unlike smaller western towns where tradition lay heavy on the order of things, Salt Lake was a bustling, modern community that seemed to be expanding as hard and as fast as brick could be fired and lumber milled. Even women worked here. The fact that the café employed a waitress instead of a waiter proved that much. So Violet Sigmond, under whatever name, could easily find work in Salt Lake City. In most places a single girl was restricted to very few job opportunities: taking in laundry, making clothes or hats. Very little else was respectable. And for that matter, there was nothing carved in stone that said Violet Sigmond had to be acting the respectable young lady after she ran away from home. If she'd gone to whoring it certainly wasn't something her brother would know about. So the girl could be just about anywhere now, doing damn near anything to support herself. Respectable jobs or not so respectable ones.

She'd changed her name, hadn't she? She'd pretended not to know the family friend who reported seeing her here. Was there anything else the guy'd learned that he hadn't wanted to pass along to Roy Sigmond, perhaps out of respect for Sigmond's feelings? That was always possible. It could have been that Violet had changed her name as much to protect the family honor as to hide herself once she reached the big city.

Raider frowned into the dark, oily coffee. There were things he'd rather do than chase around looking for missing persons. Almost anything would qualify on that count.

He frowned again, finished his snack and dropped a coin on the table to pay for it.

He sure hoped something interesting would break— something like, say, a nice, messy train holdup—so Pinkerton would pull him off this case and let him get back to doing what he did best.

CHAPTER SIX ·

Raider was footsore and pissed off when he got back to his hotel that evening. He wasn't mad at Roy Sigmond or at the missing Violet so much as he was pissed off with himself. He felt like he was floundering on this case. It was the sort of thing that should be easy for any operative with half a grain of sense. And probably it was. But it sure put a beating on a man's boot leather trying to track down someone in a strange town.

He'd spent the entire afternoon wandering here and there, wherever he could think that a young girl alone in a strange town might look for work, then stopping by boarding houses that catered to single women. He knew not a single thing more tonight than he had when he started out in the morning. His feet ached and his throat was dry. No one admitted to knowing either Violet Sigmond or Violet Thorn. No one had ever heard of her. All in all, Raider would not claim that this had been one of his better days.

Instead of going up to his room he angled toward the hotel bar, termed in a place this nice a gentlemen's lounge.

"Mr. Raider." The desk clerk stopped him outside the connecting door from the lobby into the lounge.

"Yeah?"

"There is a messenger waiting to see you, sir."

"For me?"

"Yes, sir." The clerk pointed to the far side of the lobby where a man was reading a newspaper. Raider couldn't see much of the fellow because of the newspaper held in front of him, but he knew it wasn't Roy Sigmond waiting there. This man was much smaller and not so well dressed.

"Thanks." Raider turned away from the badly wanted drink and crossed the lobby to stand in front of the man with the paper. "You wanted to see me?"

The man carefully folded his newspaper and laid it aside. "You're Raider?"

"Uh-huh."

The messenger was in his late teens or early twenties, a very slightly built young man wearing a threadbare suit, sloppily knotted tie, a derby hat, and wire-rimmed spectacles. For all of that, though, he did not look like anybody's office boy. There was something about him, something in his eyes, that said his clothing was a deliberate attempt at misdirection and that this mild, meek, young fellow could be very salty if he wanted. A telltale bulge under his left armpit added to that impression. He was packing iron there. Raider somehow doubted that very many errand boys in Salt Lake City had that habit.

The young messenger reached inside his coat. And found himself looking into the muzzle of a rather large Colt revolver. The fellow didn't flinch. He ignored the gun and looked past it to Raider's cold, level eyes. A small smile thinned his lips. "No harm intended, Mr. Raider." His smile didn't waver as he extracted a pasteboard folder from an inner pocket and held it for Raider to see.

Raider grunted and slipped the Colt back into its holster. He glanced over his shoulder, but no one in the hotel lobby had noticed the quick, silent interplay.

"Mr. Sigmond asked me to deliver this to you and to get a progress report from you." He extended the folder.

Raider took it with his left hand. "My name is Caldwell, Mr. Raider. Ira Caldwell. I work for Mr. Sigmond too."

Raider didn't particularly care for that "too" business, but it wasn't a point he wanted to argue. "No mister attached to my name," was all he said. "Just Raider will do."

Caldwell nodded. He was still smiling. "Kinda nervous, aren't you, Raider?" He glanced at the worn butt of the revolver.

"No. Just kinda cautious." There was something about Ira Caldwell that Raider did not particularly like. He had no inclination at all to invite the young man to have a drink with him.

Caldwell shrugged. "Whatever. So. Do you have anything to report to Mr. Sigmond yet?"

"Just that I'm working on it."

"I'll tell him."

"You do that, Caldwell."

The young messenger tilted his head slightly. His eyes narrowed as he gave Raider a look of long, silent speculation. Then he smiled again, the expression not coming anywhere near his eyes, and said, "I don't think I ever met a Pink before."

"We're mostly human," Raider said.

Caldwell stood. "Yeah, well, that's always good t' know, isn't it."

Raider said nothing.

"You know where to find Mr. Sigmond when you have something to tell him."

"Uh-huh." On a hunch Raider added, "You figger you shoulda been asked t' find the lady, Caldwell?"

Caldwell gave him an innocent, boyish grin. "Me? Naw. I wouldn't know how to go about it, Raider." He laughed. "I'm just an odd-job messenger."

Raider didn't believe that for a minute. Not with a big-bore revolver in a shoulder holster, he wasn't. "Whatever you say."

"I'll be seeing you again, Raider."

"Lookin' forward to it," Raider said dryly.

"Yeah. Me too."

Caldwell walked away, and Raider turned back toward the bar again.

Interesting, he was thinking, the kind of people who ran errands for Roy Sigmond.

Over a beer, though, he decided it probably wasn't so unusual after all. A rich man with gold or silver mines might well want, or even need, bodyguards around him. Probably that was all it was.

Young Ira Caldwell sure did rub Raider the wrong way, though. There was something about him—

Raider shrugged the feeling off and reached for a pickled egg on the free lunch spread. Ira Caldwell wasn't his problem. Violet Sigmond/Thorn was.

CHAPTER SEVEN

The pasteboard folder Ira Caldwell had delivered was going to be a very big help.

The folder contained a formally posed tintype showing a handsome young woman wearing an expensive gown and with her hair done in a severe style. Violet Sigmond.

Despite the stiff, solemn posing required in a tintype Raider could see the softness and the warmth of the girl. Hints of what she must be like came through even under those strained circumstances. She looked like a girl who enjoyed life and laughter, a girl who liked to tease and play jokes. And not a girl accustomed to the darker side of living. She looked wholesome and friendly.

No point in looking for this one in the cribs or cathouses, Raider realized. A girl like this would never think to go there even if she was starving. Violet Sigmond looked like a sweet, gay, thoroughly nice young lady.

Raider examined the picture again and decided he would like Violet when he finally met her.

Sigmond said she was twenty. In the tintype she looked even younger, although the bright, unfaded condition of the picture indicated that it couldn't have been taken long before she ran away from home.

In the picture she looked happy and completely untroubled. Whatever the problem had been between

Violet and her father, it did not show here. Raider found himself wondering about that, and quite frankly hoping that whatever it was that drove Violet away from home was not something that had changed her from the way she'd been when this picture was taken.

Oddly, seeing the tintype of Violet gave Raider a different outlook on the job he was doing for her brother. As far as Roy Sigmond was concerned, Raider's view was only that this was something that had to be done until something better came up. But if his finding Violet would help her, would help her retain the sweet softness that was so readily apparent in the portrait, well, that was something else again. Raider found himself wanting to help this girl, and he could do that by finding her and returning her to her family and to her inheritance.

He grunted to himself and tucked the folder away carefully so he would not bend or damage the tintype it held. Now, perhaps, with the portrait to show, he would be able to find the girl no matter what name she might be using.

He shaved and dressed and ate quickly the next morning. For the first time since he'd been assigned this case he was anxious to find Violet and do something that would help her.

He was whistling and his step was light and swift as he left the hotel that morning in search of Violet Sigmond.

CHAPTER EIGHT

"Certainly I know her." The shopkeeper blinked and gave Raider a look of suspicion, obviously regretting now that he'd been so quick to admit to knowing the girl in the tintype.

Raider was just as quick to smile and reassure the man. He produced his Pinkerton's credentials and displayed them. "I don't figger t' cause the lady any trouble," he said, "an' I'm no masher. Though I admire yer caution in thinkin' 'bout her best int'rests." He kept the smile just as warm and sincere and friendly as he could manage, which was considerable when he chose to use it that way. He could also be one cold, intimidating son of a bitch when the need arose, of course, but this guy needed the friendly treatment to open him up now that Raider knew he'd struck gold in this out-of-the-way little greengrocer's.

It had been a struggle getting here, too. Three more days of walking and talking in all the likely places—every damned hotel, residential hotel, ladies' boarding house, laundry, café or restaurant—and never a nibble on Roy Sigmond's tintype. It'd been a bitch of a long time, but the payoff was in sight.

Raider gave the grocer another radiant smile and

sidled a little closer to show that they were good buddies now and both of them concerned about Violet's best interests.

"The thing is," Raider told the guy in a low, confidential tone, secrets shared and all that, "the lady has quite a nice little inheritance comin' t' her. The Pinkerton Agency's been hired t' find her so's she can collect it."

That was, in fact, no lie.

"So could you tell me where t' find her?"

That one right there was the kicker. It was what all the searching had been about.

The shopkeeper glanced around to make sure no one overheard, Raider's conspiratorial manner apparently contagious. "That's Missus Thorn, mister. Les's wife."

Raider frowned. Why the hell was that name familiar? Then it came to him. The clerk at City Hall. The guy had come up with nothing on a Violet Thorn but had given him an address for a Lester Thorn. He'd been told about the name Violet Thorn, of course. But as an alias. It quite honestly hadn't occurred to him—he was cussing himself now for his own oversight—that Violet Sigmond could have gotten herself married in the past few months to a man named Thorn. He hadn't thought to check the marriage records, damn it, when he was at City Hall. He'd had the information he needed right from day one and hadn't known it.

"She shops here," the grocer was going on. "Comes in regular as can be on Tuesdays and Fridays. Early evening shopper generally. Except this is Wednesday, and now that I think about it she didn't come in yesterday." He shrugged.

"And her husband?" Raider asked.

The man shrugged again. "I've seen him but couldn't claim that I know him. Gentile fella." For a moment Raider thought the man had said "gentle," then real-

ized the difference here in the heart of Mormon country. "A carpenter, I think he is. Of course it was
Missus Thorn does all their shopping." He frowned. "I
wonder why she wasn't in yesterday. Hope she hasn't
taken her business someplace else."

"I hope not," Raider said agreeably. He smiled
again. "Tell you what, neighbor. You been real helpful. If this all comes right, an' it sure should, I'll make
sure Miz Thorn knows you helped point th' way t' her
an' Mr. Thorn gettin' that money."

That prospect pleased the grocer enormously. The
moment of concern fled, and he was suddenly eager to
be of help. "What I could do," he volunteered, "is
have my delivery boy take you to the Thorn place.
That's the way I do my business, you see. The ladies
stop in and drop their grocery lists off for me to fill,
then I get their orders all together and have everything
delivered right to their doors. It's a really wonderful
convenience, them not having to lug boxes and bags
themselves."

"I'm sure it is," Raider agreed pleasantly, not really
caring if this guy's customers carried their own purchases or not.

"Billy is out on a delivery now, but he should be
back here any moment now." After Raider's offer of a
good word on his behalf the guy didn't want to take any
chances on the Pinkerton operative reneging on the
deal. If anything, he wanted Raider to be all the more
in his debt as a guarantee toward the greengrocer's
future business prospects, particularly with a customer
who would be in the bucks and presumably buying
more and better produce than ever before. Raider understood that quite well and didn't mind it in the
least.

"Here. You can sit on the stool right over there. And
help yourself to the pickle barrel or some crackers if
you like. No charge. My pleasure to be of assistance."
The grocer shepherded Raider to the favored spot, help-

fully flipped back the hinged lids on the nearby barrels of sour pickles and hard crackers and hurried off toward the storeroom in search of his delivery boy.

Raider crossed his legs and waited patiently for them to return. He'd wasted some time of course, nothing about that to be proud of, but Roy Sigmond's case was as good as done with now and Allan Pinkerton would certainly be happy with the promised bonus payment.

At least so he thought.

CHAPTER NINE

Raider thanked the boy who had led him to the tall, blocky building set beside the wide irrigation canal— dammit, he remembered something about that City Hall clerk mentioning the canal now—and tipped the boy a dime.

"They live upstairs in the back," the kid told him helpfully. "There's stairs around back an' a shed where the mister does his cabinet makin' an' like that."

Raider thanked the boy and left him on the street, making his way alone to the rear of the apartment house.

Why in hell hadn't he thought to come here to begin with? The damned case'd been laid right in his lap and he ignored it all this time. There was no way a man could feel good about that. Fortunately no harm had been done.

He passed by the shed where Les Thorn did his cabinet making. The shed doors were closed, and there was no sound of activity inside. Violet's husband must be out on a job somewhere.

Raider noticed that the doors were secured by a hasp, but there was no padlock in place. Instead, a hefty bolt with a head too large to slip through had been dropped in place to keep the doors from blowing open in Thorn's absence. Honest folks in Salt Lake, Raider figured, if a carpenter could leave his tools like that. That was nice.

32

He mounted the outside stairway two treads at a time. The stairs were flimsy and in poor repair. Raider hoped Lester Thorn wasn't the carpenter responsible for them or he and his young bride must be short on groceries. One thing for sure, though. Quick as Roy Sigmond found his sister, Mr. and Mrs. Lester Thorn would be able to move into a place a sight better than the apartment house called The Gates.

From the landing at the top of the stairs Raider could see where the building got its name. Sixty or seventy yards behind it at a fork in the irrigation canal there was a set of flow gates.

Raider tapped lightly on a door leading into the second story of the building. There was no answer so he cupped his hands at the glass to keep the reflection off and peered inside. No wonder no one had answered. The door led not into the Thorn apartment but to a common hall that ran the length of the building. More doors along that corridor gave access to the apartments on either side. The hallway door was unlocked, so Raider let himself in.

There were six doors inside, three on each side, so presumably there were six apartments on each floor. Three floors to the building. And the construction of the place was crude and cheap. Somebody was making a nice profit on this operation, and it was the sort of thing that would keep on paying year after year. Good business practice, Raider supposed, but nothing that he envied the owner. A deal like this would sure tie a man down.

There were metal number plates affixed to the inside doors but no name cards. He had no way of knowing which of the places belonged to the newly married Thorns. The boy, Billy, had said Violet lived at the back. Raider tried knocking on the doors of both rear apartments but got no answer at either of them. Apparently Violet, and her neighbor too, were out somewhere. He cussed and complained a little. But a bit longer wasn't going to make much difference.

He went outside into the fresher air and the sunshine and settled himself on the top step of the staircase. Patience was something a man had to accept in this business, and he was prepared to wait right there until the cows came home. Or the Thorns, whichever happened first.

Sigmond had said Raider wasn't to contact Violet; he wanted to do that himself. But the girl wasn't actually located until Raider saw her for himself and knew for sure that Mrs. Thorn was the former Violet Sigmond. What he figured he could do was simply tip his hat and and get a good look at her when she came up the stairs, wait to see which apartment she went into, and then go over to the Grand Simeon and let Roy Sigmond know that his sister'd been found.

Raider hadn't seen Sigmond himself—or Eleanor—since he got to Salt Lake. So this afternoon was going to be a double pleasure. Not only would he have a reason to chat with pretty Eleanor again—he started getting horny just thinking about Sigmond's gorgeous wife—he would also get that damned Caldwell off his back. The guy showed up regular as clockwork at Raider's hotel each evening to collect Sigmond's daily progress report, and Raider didn't like Sigmond's bodyguard a lick better now than he had the first time he laid eyes on the man.

For once it was going to be practically a relief to get back to Chicago and whatever else Allan Pinkerton or Wagner had in mind for his next assignment. Whatever it was, it almost had to be more interesting than this one had been.

He was still sitting there at the top of the stairs, musing quietly to himself, when a young woman came around the back of The Gates and started up the stairs.

CHAPTER TEN

Raider stood and pulled his Stetson off. With his other hand he reached out and relieved the woman of the heavy sack that was slipping out of her fingers. Her chin was low with fatigue and he doubted that she had so much as seen him on the stairs until he moved to help her with the burden.

"Oh." She jumped a little and would have dropped the bag if he hadn't had a good grip on it already.

"Ma'am." When she looked up at him, startled for that first brief instant, he saw that this was not the woman in Roy Sigmond's tintype. She was young, true, and she was pretty enough, but she wasn't Violet Sigmond Thorn. "Didn't mean t' give you a fright, ma'am."

She smiled gratefully and motioned toward the sack. "Thank you for saving that from a fall. I have eggs in there."

Raider grinned. "Actually, ma'am, I think I'm the one woulda made you drop it. Sorry 'bout that."

She shrugged and gave him another smile as she mounted the last few steps to the landing. Once they were on a level he could see that she was a small woman, not more than five foot one and that would be if she fudged it by stretching a little. Wisps of dark brown hair were escaping from her bun, and her eyes were a soft, sandy brown that was almost tan in color. She looked like she'd had a frazzled morning of it and was about worn out.

"I can take that now." She extended her hand for the sack.

"Be glad t' carry it in for you, ma'am."

She gave him a closer look, seemed to decide there was nothing threatening about this tall, handsome man, and nodded. "Thank you, sir." She sounded very much relieved to not have to carry her groceries any farther.

"No, 'sir' to it, ma'am. Name's Raider." He bowed slightly, the gesture hampered because the landing was small and they were standing quite close together. The movement brought him close enough to her that he could tell she smelled nice. Fresh-scrubbed and feminine although the scent was entirely her own. She was wearing no perfume or toilet water.

"I am Melly Dvorchekha, Mr. Raider. And I thank you." She was grinning now as he accepted the information but hoped he wouldn't have to try and wrap his tongue around it. She seemed to know good and well what he was thinking. The Melly part could be short for any number of names. But Dvorchekha?

"I know," she said lightly. "It sounds like a hiccup, doesn't it?"

Raider laughed but didn't disagree. It did at that.

"This way please, Mr. Raider."

"Just Raider," he corrected.

"As you wish then."

He opened the door to the apartment house hall and held it for her, then followed her inside. The hallway seemed dim and cool after the bright sunshine outside.

Melly Dvorchekha fumbled in her handbag for a latchkey and let herself into the apartment unit at the right-hand rear of The Gates. Which answered something for Raider right there. The Thorns had to live in the left-hand apartment across the hall from the Dvorchekhas. He followed her inside with the sack of groceries.

"Where would you like these, Miz Dv—uh—ma'am?"

She laughed again and pointed to a counter near the tiny stove.

If the Thorn's place was anything like this one, and it pretty much had to be, Roy Sigmond's little sister wasn't exactly living in the lap of luxury these days.

The place was shabby, its walls poorly lathed, and the cheap wallpaper peeling. The furniture was threadbare, and there wasn't very much of it. The apartment seemed to consist of just two rooms, the one where Raider was standing serving multiple uses as kitchen, parlor, and dining room all rolled into one. An inside door presumably led to a bedroom. Raider had no idea where the bathroom would be if there was one. Probably everybody shared a common facility somewhere on the floor.

Sigmond wasn't going to like this. But then it would probably give him all the more pleasure to be getting his sister out of it. Melly Dvorchekha either didn't mind her surroundings or pretended not to in front of a stranger.

Raider put the bag where she indicated and stepped back politely. "Well, I better step outside again, ma'am. Sorry I almost made you drop th' eggs."

"You are waiting for someone?"

"Yes, ma'am." He did not explain any further. Sigmond wanted to make that first contact with Violet himself. If Raider mentioned who he wanted to see the neighbor could well tell Violet about the visitor and worry her. Sigmond'd said something about her being nervous about strangers and easily frightened. Raider didn't want to do that.

"You very likely shall have a long wait then," Melly said. "Everyone else in the building works during the day. I doubt anyone will be home until evening."

"Thank you for tellin' me, ma'am."

"But you'll wait anyway?"

"Yes, ma'am."

She tilted her head to one side and gave him a second inspection. "I could offer you some lunch if you intend to wait. I—" she hesitated. Then her jaw firmed, and she smiled again. "Of course I can offer you a bite to eat."

Raider guessed that the first offer had been made on an impulse, but there was a subtle note of something—defiance?—in her voice the second time she mentioned it.

He guessed that she was on a tight budget and might be getting herself in some trouble by giving a plate of food away.

"That's mighty nice o' you, ma'am. I'd be glad t' pay you for the meal, o' course."

She frowned, and he could see that she was caught somewhere between convention and need. The polite thing to do was to refuse his offer of pay for the meal. But she needed the money.

"Please," he added. Then with a smile said, "It's expense account money, anyhow. The Pinkerton Detective Agency will be payin' for it." Hell, with all the great, gaudy wad of cash Roy Sigmond had given him, Raider couldn't get rid of it all before the close of this case now if he threw it away by the handful.

That information tipped the balance for Melly Dvorchekha. She looked both relieved and pleased. "Thank you."

"My thanks t' you, ma'am."

"You can put your coat and hat over there," she said now that the question was settled. "I'll get started on your meal."

Raider hung his things on a peg sticking out from the wall and sat rather gingerly on a chair that looked like it belonged in the stovewood box. He hoped to hell the thing didn't collapse under him. Fortunately it held together at least this one more time.

Melly began pulling her groceries from the bag Raider had brought inside. No wonder the thing had been so heavy. Nearly all she'd bought were cheap, bulky items like potatoes, cornmeal, and rice. There was one tiny poke inside the bag that she handled with almost reverent care. Those would be the eggs she'd mentioned, he guessed, but judging from the size of the bag there couldn't be more than four or five eggs in the cloth poke.

"Would eggs and fried potatoes be all right, Mr. Raider?"

"The fried taters'd be just fine, ma'am, but please don't fix me no eggs. I'm allergic to 'em," he lied.

She gave him a look that said she found that statement just about as truthful as it actually was, but she didn't insist. She transferred the eggs—there were four of them—to a bowl and set it carefully inside a cupboard, then tipped water from a bucket into a large pan and began scrubbing some potatoes. Apparently she wasn't going to have an egg for herself either.

"I could fill that bucket for you, ma'am. If you'd tell me where."

She looked genuinely grateful for the offer, and no wonder. The pump was outside at the side of the building. And a bucket of water is a burden for a small woman to carry.

While Melly started a fire in the stove Raider made trips down and back with the bucket until he had filled the hot water reservoir on the side of the stove, a tiny tin cistern on the counter, and the bucket itself. He was about half winded by the time he'd done all that and was pleased that lunch was ready by then even if it was only a bait of potatoes fried in some much-used grease.

"You can't know—"

"My pleasure, ma'am," he interrupted.

When they had both eaten Melly seemed quite delighted to be able to draw hot water from the stove's reservoir for the washing up. Apparently she wasn't used to having so much on hand at any one time.

"Let me dry those, ma'am, as you get 'em washed," Raider offered.

"Oh, I couldn't—"

"Aw, I don't mind. Really." He stepped up beside the copper lined sink and snagged a ragged towel off a hook.

Melly had rolled the sleeves of her dress up so she could put her hands into the dishpan. Raider glanced down at them and began to scowl.

Melly Dvorchekha saw where he was looking. Her pretty face flushed a bright, shamed red, and she spun away from the sink and began to cry.

CHAPTER ELEVEN

Raider stood with the dish towel in his hands, feeling awkward and angry at the same time. More angry than awkward, he decided after a moment. Furious, in fact.

This wasn't his woman to worry about. Hell, he didn't even really know her. But dammit, no son of a bitch was entitled to do that to a nice, pretty little woman like Melly Dvorchekha.

Melly's forearms were dark and purpled with bruises and scabbed with old abrasions and some not so old.

Raider's scowl softened; he stepped forward to take Melly by the shoulders and turned her to face him. He pulled her closer and wrapped his arms around her trembling shoulders in an effort to give her some comfort, a shoulder to cry on.

Damn the SOB anyway who would do a thing like that to a very nice woman.

Raider stood there silently and let her cry it out. She was shivering now, and he could feel the moist heat of her tearful breath through the cloth of his shirt. She pressed her face tight against his chest and sobbed for what seemed a long time.

"I want you t' tell me 'bout it," Raider said in a low, cold voice when she seemed to have calmed a little.

"I couldn't." Her voice, so cheerful and pleasant before, was almost a whimper now.

"There's some things that just ain't right," Raider told her. "What's been done t' you is one of 'em."

"I—I couldn't." She pulled away from his chest and tipped her chin high so she could look up at him. She tried to smile, but the attempt was pathetically weak. "It's really my own fault, you see. I deserve to be—be—punished." A bright jewel-like tear welled out of the corner of her left eye and rolled down her already teartracked cheek. "Honestly. I ought to be—you know." She dropped her eyes away from his.

Raider took her wrist and gently but insistently turned it over so he could see her forearm. He pushed the sleeve of her dress higher. Her entire arm was covered with bruises and welts. It was the same on the other arm. Coldly now, he reached around and touched the small of Melly's back. She winced and jerked away from the light contact. He could guess what her back must look like. It would be worse than her arms.

"Tell me," he said, not at all gently this time.

Melly shook her head, panic reflecting stark and quick in her soft eyes. "I can't," she breathed. "He would—you don't know. I just can't."

Raider nodded. She'd already told him quite enough, actually. The son of a bitch who'd done this to Melly wasn't only cruel, Raider realized. He was a cold, calculating bastard about his cruelty.

Raider tipped Melly's chin up and examined her face, turned her and looked closely at the back of her neck, then at her unmarked hands and wrists.

Her cheap dress buttoned high at the throat. Raider turned the pretty little woman to face him and unfastened the buttons at her throat. Melly closed her eyes but did not try to turn away. He meant no indecency with her, and she knew it.

He had to open only three buttons before he exposed a dark, vivid bruise on her chest.

One cold, calculating cocksucker, Raider thought. There wasn't a single mark on Melly Dvorchekha that could be seen when she was dressed, but as far as Raider could tell there was damned little of her body that wasn't battered otherwise.

Something like this wasn't done by a man who was mad at her. It hadn't been done in heat, and the bastard hadn't even the excuse of being drunk. The man who'd systematically and brutally and repeatedly beaten Melly Dvorchekha knew exactly what he was doing. His mind wasn't clouded by drink or opium or anger or anything else. And the beatings weren't the only way he abused her either. She'd actually told Raider that the abuse was her own fault. That she deserved it. The man had made her so frightened and confused that she either believed that herself or was too scared to admit to anything else.

Even in the little things, Raider was realizing, this guy was a first class asshole. The battered little woman had to lug all the water for the household. She got damn little to eat while the hairy-chested asshole of the house got the best of what there was.

Raider could feel a cold fury forming in his gut like a block of gritty ice. He definitely wanted to meet Mr. Dvorchekha, he realized. Maybe see how the gentleman acted when it was a man standing in front of him. It takes one low form of life to beat up on a defenseless woman in Raider's considered opinion. With any kind of luck, though, Mr. Dvorchekha would be the type to try and bully grown men too. Raider smiled thinly. He damn sure hoped so.

He regained control of himself and stroked Melly's tear stained cheek gently. "I didn't mean t' embarrass you, ma'am. I'm sorry."

"You won't—won't cause any—commotion? About this? I mean, Anton would just—" She shuddered and couldn't finish the sentence. Likely she was afraid to finish the thought in her own mind too. She was scared half to death of the ape who'd done these things to her.

"No, ma'am," Raider lied in a soft voice. "I wouldn't want t' bring you harm." That, at least, was pure truth. He smiled to soften the lie he'd told her.

"Quick as I see the Thorns 'cross the hall there I'll be gone. I promise you I won't say nothin' 'bout this. Not to a livin' soul."

She gave him a worried, searching look. Then nodded. "I accept your word, Mr. Raider. Thank you." She seemed genuinely grateful to him.

Damn that son of a bitch anyhow, Raider was thinking. But he would keep his word. He wouldn't say anything about what he'd seen here. He'd made no promises about not doing anything.

And it was nice, he thought, that Melly had mentioned her husband's name. Anton. Anton Dvorchekha. Now Raider wouldn't have to worry her by asking.

He pulled out some of Roy Sigmond's expense money and laid a crisp fifty on the kitchen table beside his greasy plate. It was rather extreme payment for a single lunch, but he suspected Melly might be having need of a few extra dollars soon. After all, it was entirely possible that her husband wouldn't be able to work for a while.

"I'll be going now, ma'am." He retrieved his coat and hat from the wall peg and was at the apartment door when Melly stopped him there.

"Mr. Raider."

"Yes, ma'am?"

"You said you were waiting to see the Thorns?"

"Yes, ma'am?"

"They left, Mr. Raider."

"Ma'am?"

"They packed up all their things and left. Two nights ago, I think it was. Or three? I can't remember for sure. Les sold some of his tools, I know that, and they bought a wagon to haul what was left. Violet didn't tell me where they were going." She frowned. "I think they didn't know. Just that they were leaving here, but neither of them ever said where or why. Violet came by just long enough to tell me good-bye and—give me a hug."

Melly started to cry again. "Violet was the only friend I had here. She—knew, you see. I miss her dreadfully."

"If I see her I'll tell her that," Raider said. "They never said why they were movin'?"

"No, but I'm sure they were leaving the city. They wouldn't have bought a wagon otherwise."

"Yes, ma'am."

"Just that very morning Violet and I had made plans to shop together. We nearly always did, of course. And she would have me over sometimes and we would have tea and—everything would be so nice then." Melly's tears were coming harder again.

"If I see 'em, ma'am, I'll tell her how much you miss her," Raider promised.

"Ask her to write?"

"Yes, ma'am. I will."

He stood in the doorway for a moment, looking back at the pretty, sweet, miserable little woman who deserved so much better than the hand she'd been dealt.

There wasn't anything else he could say. There was no comfort he could give that would count for anything.

He could accomplish nothing more here.

"Goodbye, ma'am." He touched the brim of his Stetson. "I won't forget the promises I made t' you."

Melly squared her shoulders and lifted her chin, a small, bright, nice woman who was making the best of an impossible situation.

"Thank you, Mr. Raider. Good-bye."

He nodded and turned toward the stairs. His concentration at the moment was on Melly Dvorchekha and her husband Anton, and it scarcely got through to him that he was going to have to start his search for Les and Violet Thorn all over again.

That, though, was something he could think about later. This afternoon there was something else he wanted to do.

CHAPTER TWELVE

It took a little asking around in the neighborhood, but it was no great trick to find out where Anton Dvorchekha worked. The pity was that it wasn't so easy to locate Violet Sigmond Thorn. But that could come later, Raider figured.

Melly's woman-beating husband was a cobbler in a shop half a mile or so from The Gates. That was, Raider reflected as he ambled in that direction, a trade that could be learned in several different state pens he could think of offhand. Not that there was necessarily any connection, but still—

There was a customer in the shop ahead of him, an elderly woman with a pair of old-fashioned and much worn high-laced shoes to be repaired. Raider waited while the man behind the counter took her shoes and assured her they would be repaired and ready for her before next Sunday.

While he waited, Raider eyed the man at the counter. He wasn't what Raider would have expected. He was a good twenty years older than Melly, gray haired and slightly built, and to all outward appearances kindly and patient. He stood there and listened to a long, garrulous complaint about how little wear a body could get out of things these days and how much better shoes used to be, and never by word or action did he hint that the customer should shut up and let him get on with fixing her shoes instead of standing there listening to her bitch about them. The guy sure as hell didn't look like Raider's idea of a woman beater, but then you couldn't always tell about people's private ways by just looking at them.

Finally the old woman ran down and left the shop.

Raider stepped up to the counter. "Dv—Dvor—are you Anton?" His expression was cold.

The cobbler smiled at him. "No, sir. Anton is my assistant. Perhaps I could help you?"

Raider relaxed a little. "Sorry. I'm lookin' for Anton." He could see there was no one else working in the small shop at the moment. The workbench behind the counter was cluttered with tools and waxed thread and work in progress, but there was no one seated at the bench.

"Anton got off a half hour ago," the cobbler said apologetically. "He opens for me, you see, and I stay later in the evening to catch the after-work traffic."

"Damn. I must of passed him in the street then."

"Not unless they've put a street through the Silver Slipper since I was there last," the cobbler offered.

"Silver Slipper?'"

"A saloon. It's in the next block over. Anton generally stops there before he goes home." The cobbler's voice was carefully neutral. Careful enough to suggest disapproval of some of Anton Dvorchekha's habits.

"Mind tellin' me what the man looks like?"

"Not at all. He is—mmm—a burly sort. Not so tall as you but quite muscular. Dark brown hair and a full beard. About thirty years old. Today he's wearing black trousers and a blue shirt."

Raider's expression turned cold again. "Thanks." He wheeled and headed for the door.

"Mister," the cobbler stopped him.

"Yes?"

"You look angry. I probably shouldn't be butting in

like this, but please be careful. Anton has a temper that I would have to say is—explosive. I don't believe it would be wise to argue with him.''

Raider turned in the doorway and gave the friendly cobbler a thin smile that failed to reach his eyes. ''I don't expect there t' be much of an argument to it. But I thank you for the warnin'.'' He waved good-bye and turned down the street in the direction the cobbler had indicated.

Raider set his second beer down and leaned back. There were three men in the Silver Slipper who answered Anton Dvorchekha's description closely enough that any of them could have been the man in question. Two of them were playing pocket billiards at a table that wasn't quite level. The third was a hard, steady drinker who was propped against the bar rail.

Now that he was here, Raider was willing to be patient about finding out which of the men was Dvorchekha.

He learned it easily enough when the two at the billiards table finished their game. The loser slammed his cue stick down in anger, the chalked tip of it tearing another hole in the already tattered cloth playing surface. The winner gave his opponent a smug look. ''That's two in a row, Anton. Pay up.''

''Fuck you. We'll play again.''

''You play again. Me, I'm going home. Now pay up.'' The winner still had his cue stick in his hands. He hefted it just a fraction of an inch to show he was damn sure ready if Anton was.

Anton grumbled and scowled, but he reached into his pocket and came up with the money. The man who'd just beaten him grunted and took it.

Raider noticed that the winner didn't turn his back until Anton had left the table and gone to stand at the bar.

Apparently Dvorchekha had a reputation that spread far and wide hereabouts.

That was just fine as fine could be.

Raider left his nearly full mug sitting on the table and walked to the bar. He chose a place immediately to Anton Dvorchekha's left, very close beside him, and ordered another beer. The bartender brought it and took Raider's nickel.

Raider waited until Dvorchekha raised his mug to drink, then reached across him for the peanut bowl. His elbow jostled Dvorchekha's mug and slopped half the beer down the front of his shirt.

"Watch it," Anton snapped.

Raider gave him the most apologetic look he could muster. From a distance anyone observing them after Dvorchekha's bark would think Raider was begging the asshole's pardon. What Raider said, though, so softly that only Dvorchekha could hear, was, "Up yours, shitface." He was smiling and nodding when he said it.

Anton Dvorchekha gave him a look of blank disbelief. Apparently he too was confused by the sharp contrast between the way Raider looked and the words Dvorchekha thought he'd heard.

Just to make sure there was no misunderstanding between them, Raider smiled and added, "'Outa my way, prick."

Dvorchekha believed it that time. His face flushed a dark, ugly red, and he let out a roar.

Raider'd hoped the SOB would react if he wasn't given time to think about backing down. He got his wish.

Anton Dvorchekha swung his beer mug at Raider's head with another outraged bellow. The beer that had been left in it sprayed the length of the bar when Raider ducked easily under Dvorchekha's sweeping fist, bringing yelps of protest from the other drinkers there.

As Raider ducked under the intended blow he sank a left and then a hard right into Dvorchekha's belly.

Anton grunted and went pale as the breath was driven out of him. The man's arms and shoulders were thick with muscle, but his gut was vulnerable. Raider hit him two more quick ones and danced away.

Behind him there was a clatter of chairs overturning as the patrons in the Silver Slipper hurried out of the way and gleeful shouts calling people in off the street to see the fight.

Dvorchekha reeled backward, stopped short at the bar and launched himself forward in a rush.

One ham-sized fist lashed out at Raider's head.

Raider sidestepped the blow, moved in and landed a stinging shot onto Dvorchekha's ear.

As big and powerful looking as he was, Anton Dvorchekha was a clumsy cocksucker. He stumbled and went to his knees.

Raider stepped back and gave Dvorchekha time to get up. He wanted to give him a thorough beating, but he didn't want any of the witnesses—there were so many of them by now that the two combatants were surrounded as closely as if they'd been in a prize fighting ring—to be able to cry foul afterward. As it stood right now everyone would be convinced that it was Dvorchekha who had started the fight, and Raider wanted to keep it that way. Any claims to the contrary Anton might make later would be taken as just so much sour grapes.

Dvorchekha stayed on hands and knees for a moment. He slung his head from side to side like a wounded buffalo, and a few splatters of blood flew. Raider's last punch had split the lobe of his right ear. Anton seemed startled and all the more pissed off when he realized he was bleeding. He came off the floor in another rush then, feinting with his right and trying to bury his left in Raider's belly.

Raider twisted out of the way of the punch and clubbed Anton behind the head. Dvorchekha was off balance again, and the blow drove him facedown onto the floor.

Amid the yelling and shouted encouragement around them Raider could hear some laughter now. Probably Dvorchekha could hear it too. If Anton didn't come off the floor and win this one now he was going to have to find another neighborhood saloon. Even so it was likely that the story would follow him anywhere he went.

Raider set himself and waited calmly.

Dvorchekha knew better than to rush Raider again. He came to his knees, then slowly to his feet. His eyes darted between the icy control of the tall, lean man who faced him and the screaming excitement of the crowd that surrounded them. For a moment he looked worried. Then the concern was replaced by a renewed fury. He took a deep breath and flexed his genuinely impressive muscles, then dropped into a poor semblance of a boxer's crouch and shuffled forward.

This time there was no rush, though. This time he came in cautiously, with his fists raised and his expression hard. Like it or not—and he didn't—he was in this fight all the way now, and he knew it.

Raider moved forward to meet him, giving himself room to maneuver backward without running into the virtually solid wall of spectators who enclosed them. He did not want to let Anton Dvorchekha get his hands on him. He'd finagled it into a punching contest, but he would be in deep shit if the fight degenerated into a wrestling match. Dvorchekha's muscle and blocky build would hold all the advantages there. To make sure Anton didn't have time enough to think of that, Raider darted forward with a pair of swift jabs and a hard right cross that snuck around Dvorchekha's inexpert guard and split his left cheek open.

Dvorchekha roared again, forgot all his resolve about protecting himself, and came on in another futile rush.

The man was such a poor fighter, despite his size and his belligerence, that Raider was able to play to the crowd with a wink as he leaned low, left his foot stuck out in Dvorchekha's path, and once again sent the big man spilling into the sawdust on the saloon floor.

Dvorchekha's fall was greeted with howls of laughter and some rude, indeed several impossible, suggestions.

Anton lay there, his thick chest heaving as he gasped for breath. Blood from his ear and cheek soaked into the sawdust.

Raider loomed tall and ready above him. Despite the beating that Dvorchekha had already taken, Raider was unruffled and unmarked. His shirttail hadn't even pulled out of his belt. His expression, though, was as cold and hard as it had been at the beginning.

"Look at that pussy layin' there," someone in the crowd shouted. "Look at 'im. Not so big now, eh, Anton?" There was enough venom in the voice to make Raider believe the crowing spectator had been whipped by Dvorchekha some time in the past and was reveling now in seeing the tables turned.

"Pussy Dvorchekha," another voice shouted.

Anton groaned and hunched forward a little in an attempt to come to his feet once again.

Raider moved forward, ready to do his level best to finish Dvorchekha now with one powerful swing.

This time, though, Dvorchekha didn't lunge forward. This time he rocked back, straightened in a panicked lurch and came up with his right hand sweeping not toward Raider's chin but very low, just at belt level.

Barely in time Raider caught the glint of lamplight on polished steel as Dvorchekha's fist raced toward his belly. Raider sucked in his gut and tried desperately to arrest his forward motion.

Dvorchekha's knife slashed viciously out. The blade clattered and scraped across the steel buckle on Raider's gunbelt, then sliced onto the leather and away.

"No!" someone shouted.

"The son of a bitch's got a knife."

Raider wasn't listening. He let Dvorchekha's momentum swing him half around, then Raider stepped forward and kicked the man in the side of the head as hard as he could.

Dvorchekha grunted.

There was a soft, ugly popping sound as cartilage or bone let go.

Anton Dvorchekha dropped face down once more. For the last time now. His body was as limp and lifeless as that of a poleaxed shoat.

The room full of shouting men became instantly silent.

"Jesus," someone muttered, the muted word loud in the oppressive quiet of the crowd.

"Yeah," someone else whispered.

Raider could see more than one man in the crowd crossing himself hastily. They had all come to see a fight, not a killing, and the sight of Anton Dvorchekha's bloody, battered body frightened them.

Hell, it startled Raider too, even if it was a long way from scaring him. He simply hadn't expected any such thing.

His kick, delivered in reflexive defense after Dvorchekha tried to knife him, had caught the side of Dvorchekha's neck just under the ear, lodged against the shelf of his jaw and lifted the man's skull off the top of his spinal cord in very much the same manner that a properly applied hangman's knot snaps the nerve centers and delivers instant death.

You could make a case for it having been an accidental death. In a way it really was. On the other hand—

Raider looked at the men in the stilled crowd surrounding him. Very few of them were willing to meet his eyes. One though, and then another and finally more, stepped forward.

"We seen it, mister. We all seen it. We all seen the knife. You was only doing what you had to."

"Nobody coulda figured it'd kill him, mister," someone assured Raider.

"We'll tell it like we seen it."

Raider nodded this thanks. "Better send somebody to fetch the police," he said.

He sighed and accepted the beer that somebody thrust into his hands. He was apt to have a long evening ahead, explaining things to the Salt Lake City police. And the worst of it—he couldn't work up much in the way of sadness over the passing of Anton Dvorchekha— was that he didn't know now if he had just helped Melly Dvorchekha or made things worse for the young wife who was so unexpectedly a young widow.

He tipped his hat back and resettled it, then shrugged his coat sleeves back where they belonged after the exertions of the fight.

"Has somebody gone to get the police?"

CHAPTER THIRTEEN

Raider was tired, hungry, and generally pissed off when he finally got back to his hotel.

Talking to the Salt Lake City police hadn't been all that unpleasant, really, There had been half a hundred witnesses to Anton Dvorchekha's death, and all of them agreed both that Raider was acting strictly in self-defense—not entirely true, but then they didn't know that—and that Dvorchekha's death had been accidental.

Still, even though the police questioning was polite and routine, the thing dragged on for half of forever.

It was late now, Raider's belly was rumbling and gurgling with hunger from a supper hour long past, and he was thoroughly tired of people yapping at him.

If there was anything he did not need right now it was Ira Caldwell sitting in the lobby waiting for the daily report to Roy Sigmond. The first thing Raider saw when he came inside, naturally, was Ira Caldwell. There was no point in trying to ignore the little shit or to evade him. Raider'd tried that once already two nights earlier. Caldwell was persistent if he was nothing else. He came every evening without fail to find Raider and get that report, and he wasn't leaving until he had it. Raider grimaced and gave in to the inevitable. He stalked across the lobby and slumped into a chair facing Caldwell.

"Well?"

Raider took his time about answering. He didn't like Caldwell, dammit, and he wasn't going to be intimidated by Sigmond's bodyguard. Finally, grudgingly, he admitted, "I found where they been stayin'. Violet an' her husband Lester." He hadn't bothered to check the records again to see if there was a legal marriage recorded and did not intend to do so. That was between Violet and Lester the way he saw it. He'd been hired to find the lady, not check up on her morals. "But they moved. Packed up and left the city just a day or so ago."

"Where—?"

"Don't push me. When I know somethin' I'll pass it along."

Caldwell's expression said he didn't like that, but he decided not to press the issue. However, he couldn't resist adding, "It took you all this time to learn that?"

Raider gave him a long, level look and said nothing. The Widow Dvorchekha's problems and Raider's involvement in them were none of Roy Sigmond's business or Ira Caldwell's either, and Raider had no intention of saying anything about that to this greaseball with the shoulder holster.

Caldwell stood and smoothed his lapel. Raider guessed the obnoxious little man was hoping the innocent gesture would provoke him into flashing the Colt again. That was the sort of thing that would probably tickle a shit like Caldwell, but Raider wasn't going to give the guy that much satisfaction.

"Tell Sigmond I'll be movin' along first thing t'morrow. Wherever they went, I'll be behind 'em."

Caldwell grunted and turned away.

One nice thing, Raider decided. Quick as he got away from Salt Lake City, and therefore away from Roy Sigmond, he would likely also be getting away from Ira Caldwell and the reporting sessions. There was that much to be grateful for. He was beginning to hope that Lester and Violet intended to relocate a nice long piece away from here.

Raider watched Caldwell disappear into the darkness outside, then headed for the hotel restaurant to see if he could still get a meal there.

CHAPTER FOURTEEN

The next morning it took Raider several hours of asking questions of the merchants in Lester Thorn's neighborhood before he finally found the man Thorn had been working for when Les and Violet decided to pack up and move.

"Ayuh, the son of a bitch was working for me," the shopkeeper growled. He pointed toward the rear of his establishment where a wall of half finished shelving smelled of raw lumber and fresh sawdust. "You see what he left me with, don't you?"

"Damn inconsiderate," Raider sympathized.

"You better b'lieve it. An' now I don't know who I'm gonna get to come in an' finish the job."

Raider grunted and shook his head. "A man ought not t' take on a job o' work if he ain't gonna see it through."

The shopkeeper replied, "You know that, friend, an' I know that, but that damned Thorn don't know that."

"Say why he quit or where he was goin', did he?"

"Some half-assed excuse was all he gave," the unhappy merchant said. "Somethin' about his wife's health. Now is that a pisser, I ask you? Walkin' out on a man 'cause of a damn woman? I ask you?" He shook his head and growled again. "Wives. The more of 'em a man has, the worse off, is what I say. Best damn thing ever happened to me, I tell you, is when the apostles said we could only have one of 'em. Divorced two of mine that very day, and I ain't had a moment's regret for it neither.''

Raider had almost forgotten the old Mormon preference for multiple wives, abandoned when the Supreme Court demanded it in exchange for Utah's admission to the Union.

The idea of being able to take as many wives as a man could afford was dandy enough to make a man horny, but judging from this man's comment maybe it was a practice that multiplied the nagging and the bitching along with the pussy. That was something Raider hadn't thought about, and he had to hide a grin from the disgruntled shopkeeper.

''Did Thorn say anythin', though, 'bout where he was headin' for his, um, wife's health?'' Raider asked, trying to return the man's interest to the point at hand.

The merchant frowned and pulled at his chin as if the gesture would somehow jog his thought processes. ''East?'' He shrugged. ''Maybe. Got that notion somehow, but I can't rightly recollect did Thorn tell me that or did I just think it.'' He shrugged again.

''It's important that I find him,'' Raider prompted.

''Tell you who you might ask then,'' the storekeeper offered. ''Thorn bought his wagon off a friend o' mine that I pointed him to. Fella name of Beavers. He might of said something to Beavers. I'll tell you how to find 'im—''

Raider stopped on the sidewalk and looked up at the false front on the building. The place was old and run-down and didn't look like it had been in use for years except maybe for the purpose of giving rats a place to nest. But this was where the man at the store said Beavers was to be found. Raider grunted softly to himself. Hell, maybe Beavers was buying the place to fix up or something. Bad as it was, it was bigger than the quarters Beavers's stationery store was in now.

Raider stood on the sidewalk listening for a moment, but he could hear nothing that would indicate there was any activity inside.

He glanced down the alley beside the place, but there was nothing going on there either. The other side of the dilapidated building was haphazardly attached to the adjacent store, which was in a slightly better state of repair.

The front windows of the old structure were boarded over, as was the door. Raider tried to peer through the cracks to see if any lamps were burning inside. For sure no one could work in there without artificial light because no sunlight could get into the front part of the building past the boards. He could neither see nor hear anything to indicate that Beavers was in there, and he couldn't go inside without ripping the boards off the doorframe.

He was positive, though, that this was where the man had said Beavers was supposed to be.

Damned strange, he decided.

Raider went back to the alley and stepped off the boardwalk into it. Beavers obviously wasn't anywhere around the front of the place, so maybe the man was in back.

Raider kicked through the trash that littered the alley as deep as a man's boot tops and made his way toward the rear. The alley was filled with broken bottles and soggy, rotting paper and broken crates. Raider's passage dislodged a pile of pasteboard shirt boxes, and something slithered out of the light and beneath the wallboards of the old building. It was gone too quickly for him to see if it had been a snake or a rat or what. Spooky damn place, he thought.

He tromped a little louder after that to make sure anything else in the alley heard him coming and had time to move aside. Hell, there could be a catamount's lair in all the shit inside this alley and nobody would ever suspect it. He felt something close to relief when he got to the back end of the alley and broke out into the sunshine of the wagon access there.

The back of the place was boarded over too, but Raider could see a man hunkered down behind a discarded barrel. Beavers, he figured.

He started to lift a hand, intending to hail the fellow.

His gut wrenched as he realized the man behind the barrel was holding a shotgun. And the scattergun was pointing square at Raider's chest. Raider threw himself backward into the loose, rotten trash inside the alley mouth just as the shotgun roared.

CHAPTER FIFTEEN

A pellet of heavy shot ripped across the heel of Raider's boot, kicking his left leg out to the side as he fell, but most of the blast was caught by the side of the old building.

Splinters and chunks of gouged, rotten wood flew across the alley mouth, and more pellets tore into the planking on the building across the alley from the derelict old place.

Raider fell onto a squishy mattress of decaying trash, rolled and scrambled to his hands and knees.

He threw himself against the protecting bulk of the building and palmed his Remington as he moved to the back of the alley.

Quickly he reached down and picked up a scrap of limp, moldy refuse. Half a discarded shirt. He didn't throw it into the gunman's view, instead only let a few inches of it show at the corner of the building like a man incautiously exposing himself to view.

The shotgun roared a second time, slicing more wood off the planking and snatching the bit of cloth out of Raider's grasp. As soon as Raider heard the second barrel discharge he was moving forward. He cleared the alley and swung the gaping muzzle of the Remington toward the barrel where he'd seen the man with the shotgun.

The man with the now empty shotgun ducked just as

Raider fired, and the heavy slug thumped into the side of the barrel beside the place where the gunman's head had been. Stagnant rain water began to stream out of the bullet hole.

Raider cocked the Remington and took aim, but he didn't fire. The ambusher was crouched behind the barrel.

He could see the twin tubes of the shotgun barrels jutting out from the side of the water barrel. The angle of the tubes dipped sharply low, remained there a moment and then jerked upright again. Raider could hear the metallic clang as the scattergun's action latched closed. The SOB had reloaded.

Raider backed toward the alley again. If the gunman came up shooting—

He did.

Raider snapped a quick, unaimed shot in his direction to throw the ambusher's aim off, then darted behind the side of the building an instant before the shotgunner fired.

Again splinters and wood chunks sprayed across the back of the alley.

"Shit!" Raider snarled.

He held the Remington ready but did not want to make the mistake of charging into a waiting load of buckshot. A thing like that could genuinely screw up a fella's day.

On the other hand, he didn't want to turn around and walk meekly away. It's bad manners to shoot at folks. Raider wanted to discuss that point of etiquette with the gunman. He took a deep breath, backed off a few paces to give himself room for a running start and then launched himself forward, out of the alley and flat onto the ground. Roll. Twist. Bring the Remington to bear. Sight.

Shit! The guy wasn't behind the barrel any more. He was out. Moving.

Raider shifted to his left in a squirming roll, and the scattergun bellowed again. A load of heavy shot beat an elongated pattern on the ground where Raider had just been, and the gunman dashed away behind a wagon shed. Out of sight and soon out of range. Raider could hear the man's running footsteps recede even as he sprang to his feet and tried to give chase. He tripped over more of the trash that strewed the ground behind the old building and sprawled face forward, his footing and balance hindered by the fact that there was no heel on his boot. That first blast had ripped it clean away, but he hadn't taken time to particularly notice that until now. He came to his feet cussing and made a futile attempt to follow, but by now the gunman was long gone.

Worse, Raider saw as soon as he rounded the wagon shed, the ambusher had abandoned the shotgun, had dropped it and left it behind when he ran. So now he could be somewhere, anywhere, on the streets of Salt Lake with his hands in his pockets and whistling a tune as he wandered down the sidewalk, and no one would have any reason to give the son of a bitch a second glance.

Raider stopped, frowned, and gave up the chase. He hadn't gotten more than a glimpse of the man who'd just tried to shoot him. But there was something—some little nagging something—that seemed almighty familiar about the fellow in those scant few seconds.

Raider reloaded the Remington and dropped it back into its holster.

It was interesting, he thought, that even though there'd been pistol and shotgun fire back in this alley like a war'd gotten started, there wasn't anyone rushing to see what was going on. That seemed damned odd in a city as civilized as Salt Lake.

He grunted softly to himself, then turned and walked back through the alley to the street, his gait artificially forced into something like a limp by the missing boot heel. He was going to have to get that replaced before he figured on doing much more in the way of walking.

And he was going to have to do some talking to Jud Beavers too.

There wasn't any way to tell yet if it had been Beavers that shot at him. But then Jud Beavers had no way of knowing a Pinkerton operative was looking for him at the old building or wanted to talk to him about anything.

Raider stopped short and considered.

As far as he knew, there wasn't any way anybody else could've known about that either. So who was waiting for him behind that damned alley? and why?

A coincidental encounter with someone gunning for somebody else and jumping Raider by mistake? The mischance of blundering into a random crazy who just happened to be standing there with a shotgun in his hands and a yen to use it on the next guy he saw? The only thing Raider knew for sure was that he'd been shot at. And that he put mighty little credence into quirks of coincidence.

He shook his head and walked on. There just wasn't any way to work it out. Yet. He wasn't likely to forget about it, though. Or to forgive it.

Since it was the only such place he knew of in town, he headed first toward the cobbler's shop where the now deceased Anton Dvorchekha used to work. Repairs While U Wait, the sign said. That would do.

CHAPTER SIXTEEN

There was no sign of the man who'd given Raider directions to the old building. Or, more to the point, to the ambush.

Jud Beavers was behind the counter of his small shop. He was definitely not the man who'd shot at Raider. Beavers was probably in his late sixties or early seventies. He was sitting on a high stool when Raider came in, and there were a pair of stout canes propped against the wall behind him.

Raider took a moment to look around the shop before he spoke. Beavers sold pens, inks, wrapping paper, and other office and stationers' supplies. The shop was small and its shelves were scantily stocked. The scent inside it was not unlike that in a newspaper office.

"Yes, sir?" The mans's voice was thin. He sounded, and looked, on the lower fringes of health.

"Mr. Beavers?"

The old man inclined his head slightly to acknowledge the fact.

"Glad t' find you in, Mr. Beavers. Your assistant told me you was over at the other building."

Beavers blinked. "Sir?"

"I said—"

"Oh, I heard you all right, young man. My hearing is just fine, thank you." He smiled. "Although I must

66

say that is nearly all that remains unaffected by the ravages of age." He sighed heavily, then smiled again. "My point, sir, is that you must be mistaken. You see, I have no assistant. Nor any other location, business or personal. I live upstairs, and this sad remnant is the entirety of my business enterprise."

"But—" Raider frowned. The man who'd directed him to Beavers, really toward the guy with the shotgun, had been sitting outside Beavers's store, acting like an idle employee waiting for a customer to come by. But Raider had talked to him outside. He hadn't actually come in on that first visit. He'd been told Beavers was at the other place, so there hadn't been any need to come in after that. "You been here all day?" Raider asked, although he was already certain he knew what Beavers's answer would be.

"Aye. As every day." Beavers inclined his head again. Then a frown deepened the wrinkles in his face. "Although not for much longer, I fear."

"You, uh, aren't expanding t' bigger quarters, I take it?"

"Hardly, sir. Arthritis keeps me confined here. My business is falling off. I can no longer get out to make deliveries or seek orders. I'll hang on while I can. From force of habit more than hope of profit. Soon I'll have to close my doors for good."

"That's why you sold your wagon, Mr. Beavers?"

"How would you know about that, sir?"

Raider explained.

The old man was feeble but not foolish. He demanded to see Raider's Pinkerton credentials before he was willing to accept the story.

"I see," he said after examining Raider's ID. "I'm afraid you have been badly misinformed, sir. The man you spoke with earlier was no employee of mine. I've not had a hired man in more than two years now. Nor lately any need for the delivery wagon, which is why I agreed to sell it to Mr. Thorn."

"You knew Thorn?"

"I did not. He was directed to me by a friend who happened to know that I had the wagon and a mule that continued to eat whether she was used or not. The arrangement seemed an agreeable one for both parties. I sold the wagon to Mr. Thorn for cash. And if I may anticipate your next question, sir, no, Thorn did not tell me where he intended to travel from here."

Raider's disappointment must have showed.

"If it helps," Beavers volunteered, "I have the impression that Thorn intended traveling to the east. And not terribly far. The wheels would have had to be completely rebuilt by a competent wheelwright before any extensive journey, particularly in the desert climate to the south or west. I said as much to Mr. Thorn, and he told me he did not believe it would be necessary to have the spokes or the tires reset."

Raider grunted. Beavers's mind worked quite as well as his hearing still did. "And Mrs. Thorn—?"

"I did not meet the lady. Mr. Thorn came alone to make the bargain. He paid cash for the price we agreed, harnessed old Lucy, and drove away. I had no idea there was a Mrs. Thorn."

Someone did. And that someone, for reasons unknown, wanted a certain Pinkerton operative dead.

Raider shook his head.

He was just making an assumption that the ambush and the search for Violet Sigmond Thorn were connected. Maybe the two had nothing to do with each other.

A simple little thing like a missing persons case, particularly one where the person who'd gone missing wasn't wanted for anything criminal but would be helped by being located, wasn't the sort of thing to bring out gunfire.

It could well be that someone wanted on criminal charges spotted Raider nosing around Salt Lake and mistakenly figured he was the target of the search.

Either didn't know that Raider was asking after a young woman or heard it but thought it was an attempt to cover up the real reason why Raider was here.

Yeah, that could be it. Or not. Too damned early to tell.

Raider talked with Beavers a while longer, but the old man had nothing more of value to contribute.

It was interesting, though, that two different men who'd talked to Thorn before Violet and Les pulled out got the impression that the young couple was heading east.

There weren't so many routes east out of Salt Lake that Raider should have any difficulty getting on their trail again.

"You wouldn't happen t' know where a fella could hire a horse, would you?" he asked Beavers.

"As a matter of fact, Mr. Raider, I have a friend in the livery trade."

Raider smiled as the old man jotted down directions and a brief note of introduction. The response hadn't been unexpected. The merchants and businessmen of Salt Lake City, as everywhere else, operated on interlocking networks of friendships and favors swapped.

Raider figured it must be late afternoon by now. It had taken some time to get his boot heel replaced and to have his talk with Beavers. Too late now to make a start after the Thorns. He could hire the horse this afternoon, though, get a good night's sleep, and make an early start of it come morning.

Raider thanked Beavers and headed toward the livery.

CHAPTER SEVENTEEN

Raider didn't get quite as much undisturbed sleep that night as he expected. When he was eating dinner, after having settled the hired horse comfortably in the stable behind the hotel, he caught the eye of a plumply pretty waitress whose work shift ended at ten, and one thing led inevitably to another.

Not that he was complaining. Hell, relaxation was better for a fellow than sleep any day.

And Jessica certainly relaxed a fellow. Relaxed him to the point of limp exhaustion, in fact. She was a sweet, smiling, gentle little thing in the dining room but a regular wildcat when you gave her a mattress to play on. One of those flattering, encouraging females who can be brought to arousal and quick, shuddering fulfillment by no more than a deep kiss; and that goes completely berserk with some pumping and driving. A girl that receptive and happy can make a man feel nine feet tall every time he touches her and that makes him want to keep on giving her pleasures over and over again when normally he might want to just roll over and get some rest.

So it was past two in the morning before Raider finally urged her out of the sack with a pat on the ass and a last, lingering kiss.

"You're sweet," he told her when she was dressed and presentable.

"And you're a lotta man." She grinned and raised her mouth to his, checked one last time to make sure she was tucked and buttoned properly, and let herself out of the hotel room.

Jessica was a joy. Good company, good sex, and no strings attached. He wished her well as he bolted the door closed behind her and yawned his way back to the rumpled bed.

"Young couple, you say, traveling in a light wagon, no kids, three, four days back?"

Raider nodded and helped himself to a dipper of the oatmeal the man had brought him. Despite the late night with Jessica he'd gotten a predawn start this morning and was as interested in the breakfast as he was in the information right now. He'd stopped at a wayside station a dozen or so miles out the old road from Salt Lake toward Fort Bridger. Nowadays the railroad to Evanston in Wyoming Territory was the easier way to go in that direction. There hadn't been an Evanston or much of anything else between Salt Lake and Bridger when the road was first cut.

The man fingered his mustache and thought for a moment before he nodded. "Ayuh. I think I do remember those two. Nice looking young woman. Wiry, pleasant looking fella?"

"Could be them," Raider said.

"They stopped here late afternoon, it was. Watered the mule was pulling the wagon and bought a couple gallons of grain off me, but had their own eatables with them. They didn't stay here. Camped on up the way, I think. At least I seen firelight in that next bunch of trees after they drove off. What'd you say you wanted them for, mister?"

Raider hadn't said, as the station keeper likely recalled quite well.

''Her father died. The family asked me t' find her an' tell her.'' It was a partial truth.

The station keeper grunted. Raider guessed he'd been hoping for some story he could gossip about. A runaway wife or fleeing lover. Something he could embellish while he spent time near the potbelly stove this winter.

''Murdered, was he?'' He sounded hopeful.

''No. Just died.'' Raider heaped sugar onto the oatmeal and doused the mess with milk so fresh and creamy it had a smoky flavor. The fare available here was plain and cheap, plenty of profit available in the fifteen cent charge for breakfast, but it would fill the emptiness behind his belt.

''Oh.'' The station keeper shrugged.

''They didn't happen t' mention which way they was goin', did they?''

''Don't recall that they did.'' The man smoothed his mustache again. ''Not so many choices along this road, though. Best bet would be to look for 'em toward Bridger. Most folks come this road, few as they are these days, that's where they're headed.'' He shrugged. ''The rest, 'bout the only other choice is to turn off southeast an' take the road over toward the Uintas. It runs over that way an' eventually comes down again to flat ground an' on over to Brown's Hole.''

The Uinta Mountains. Hell, that was where Violet was from. From Silver Canyon in the Uintas. She and her new husband could already be heading home. She could have heard about her father dying or be going back hoping for a reconciliation with the old man.

Raider wouldn't mind a bit if Violet and Les were already busy doing for themselves what the Pinkerton Agency had been hired to do.

''How far is this crossroads?'' he asked.

''Fifteen mile,'' the man said. '''You can't miss it. There's a tumbledown barn there. Used to be a relay station, but the barn's all that's left now since the rails

come and took the trade away." He shook his head.
"Damned if I can figger out why I'm still here. Stubborn son of a bitch, I reckon." He smiled. "Hope you find that young couple, mister. Person oughta be told when their kin dies. Kin's about all any of us has that counts for anything."

Raider nodded and bent to his oatmeal while the station keeper went back to his kitchen.

CHAPTER EIGHTEEN

The crossroads was as easy to identify as the man to the south had said.

About three fourths of the old barn remained, and the part of it that was standing was sagging out of plumb. A few more winters with snow pressing down on the roof, and that would fall down too. Probably the only reason even that much of it remained was that this road was now so seldom traveled that there weren't many people stopping here and wanting firewood. Raider could see the foundation and a cracked, blackened stub of chimney where the relay station once stood. The inn had been burnt or dismantled long enough ago that there was a healthy stand of brush and some small saplings growing inside the square lines of the foundation stones.

Past the barren foundation and remnants of barn he could see a narrow set of wheel ruts leading off to the right. That would be the road to the Uintas. It might have been a thriving route at one time, but that time wasn't recent. Probably the only reason a traveler could still see where the road belonged was because it takes so long for a bare path to grow over with grass in such dry country.

He pulled the hired dun to a stop. A glance toward the sun told him it wasn't lunchtime yet, but his belly

swore that was a lie. It had been three hours since he'd
had that oatmeal, and the comfort of it was about used
up by now. Besides, Raider figured, he didn't have to
push now that it looked like Violet Thorn was likely
headed for home without him. He might as well stop
here and fix himself a meal. He could find wood and
water handy here, and there was no telling what the
conditions would be like on the little used road to the
Uintas. He'd provisioned at the way station where he
had breakfast, so he had the wherewithal. And he damn
sure had the hunger.

He reined the dun not on toward the intersection but
off the Bridger road toward the foundations of the old
relay station.

The dun's back feet hadn't cleared the roadbed before he heard the thump of wood falling on wood from
the direction of the barn. Raider's attention focused
hard and suspicious on the unexpected noise. He was
already leaning, ready to drop off on the wrong side of
the dun and put the animal's body between him and the
barn, when a puff of smoke appeared at an empty
window frame. Raider kicked free of the stirrups and
hit the ground rolling.

A bullet sizzled through the air just above the seat of
the dun's saddle half a heartbeat after Raider had cleared
the leather.

The dun horse bucked and reared and broke into a
panicked run with its tail high, leaving a trail of dust
and loud farts behind it.

Raider had the Remington already in his fist. He
scrambled to his hands and knees and dived for the scanty
cover offered by a hillock of lumpy earth and gravel.

The rifleman in the barn fired again, the bullet strik-
ing the ground short of Raider and spraying him with
dirt but doing no other damage.

He reached the cover, such as it was, and took a shot
at the barn wall immediately beside the window opening where the rifleman was hiding.

The returning sound of his slug thumping solidly into wood brought a curse to his lips. The son of a bitch who cut the boards that barn was made from cut them thick and sturdy. No pistol slug fired at long range was going to smash through those and do any damage.

Raider scuttled backward to avoid a third bullet that raised a spray of gravel from the front of the hillock.

He moved to his left, aimed and triggered a shot through the window. He had no idea where the bullet went, but he sure didn't hear anything encouraging, like screams or dying wails.

Raider changed position and fired twice more, then ducked behind the hillock and quickly shucked the empties from his cylinder to reload.

The rifle spat death toward him again, from between two cracks in the thick boards this time, but again the result was no more dangerous than some dirt and gravel flying in the air. Some of it spattered onto Raider's Stetson, and a little got into his left ear. It tickled enough to be annoying. Annoying wasn't anything compared to what he wanted to do to that asshole inside the barn.

He aimed for the gap between two warped boards and fired four shots, sweeping across the width of the back wall as far as the crack extended, then hunched low and reloaded again.

"Shit!"

He came to his feet, Remington leveled and extended. From the far side of the barn he could hear the thump and clatter of horse hooves on wood and then quickly onto hard earth.

The guy with the rifle was running.

Raider broke into a run, trying to get out to the side so the barn wouldn't be between him and the fleeing ambusher. The guy was making a straight line away from the barn and using it to block Raider's sight.

Raider ran to his right and got a glimpse of the retreating man's back. By then, though, the rifleman was well over a hundred yards away and moving as fast as his horse could go.

Raider stopped, took a deep breath and aimed a good two feet above the small of the man's back. He took a two-handed grip on the butt of the Remington, made sure his breath was controlled, and squeezed.

The big gun bucked and roared and spat out its thunder. Raider hadn't any idea where the bullet went, but it sure didn't hit the rifleman. Didn't even make him flinch.

He turned to grab the dun's reins and give chase.

The horse wasn't anywhere in sight.

After some careful searching and the uttering of a hatful of choice words, he finally spotted the horse cropping grass under some trees a good quarter mile away. By the time Raider could leg it to the dun—and catch the damn thing if it decided to get contrary on the subject—the ambusher was going to be miles away.

With a grimace and a growl Raider reloaded the Remington and dropped it back into his holster.

CHAPTER NINETEEN

Raider grumbled and complained, but there wasn't any point now in trying to start a fast chase. Not with the ambusher miles away in any direction he chose.

He tied the dun to the empty frame where the barn door once hung. It had taken him twenty minutes of sweet talk and encouragement to get within rein-grabbing distance of the miserable excuse for a livery horse. By that time he'd have preferred to shoot it than catch it, but that didn't seem bright considering how far the walk back would be.

The inside of the barn was shadowy, the gloom stippled with bright sunlight where it shone through gaps in the roof. Raider stood for a moment surveying the interior. The east wall of the structure had collapsed in the middle, but all the corners stood. There were fresh piles of manure in the northeast corner showing where a horse had been left standing. Four or five piles probably. It was hard to tell for sure because the horse had been tied short and had scattered the turds and stepped in them when it shifted its rump back and forth. Overnight anyway, Raider judged. The animal was tied there at least overnight and half of today. There were some soggy oat grains caught in the cracks of a wood slab laid in the corner where the horse had been tied. So the ambusher came here probably late yesterday and

planned far enough ahead to bring feed for his horse
with him. That did seem almighty interesting.

Raider walked over to the other side of the barn to
the window the first shots had been fired from. He
found the rifleman's empty brass. Dirt common .44-40
casings of the sort that fit probably seventy-five percent
of all the rifles and revolvers between St. Louis and San
Francisco, including his own guns. Raider wasn't going
to identify the persistent sniper by his choice of exotic
weapons. A cheap shotgun the first time and now a
.44-40 carbine.

If it was the same guy, that is. Neither time had
Raider gotten a good look at the man. He hit quickly
and unexpectedly and had sense enough to run like hell
if it didn't go his way. To try again another time? Not
an encouraging notion.

Of the man himself there was very little sign, Raider
discovered. He didn't seem to smoke or to chew, and
there weren't any liquor bottles lying around. Great.
Raider was being stalked by a puritan. Hell, there
couldn't be too many of those in the woods.

The guy did have to piss, though, just like any
ordinary human person. Raider found his latrine in the
northwest corner of the barn. He'd been there long
enough to piss several times but not long enough to
have to take a shit while he was waiting for his quarry
to show up on the road.

Raider grunted and walked back to the window again.
There was a dandy view of the road to the south. The
guy would have been able to watch Raider come in for
at least a mile and a half. Tons of time for him to get
ready.

There was another window facing the intersection of
the Bridger and Uinta roads. That one was much closer
to the barn. The shot wouldn't have been more than
forty yards. Point-blank range for a rifle but stretching
it in most men's hands for a pistol. Likely the ambusher
watched Raider come to him and planned to wait till he

reached the intersection before he fired. Either road
Raider took would have been a dead easy—literally
dead—shot for an ambusher standing inside the barn
there. Shoot for the chest if he turned onto the Uinta
cutoff or take him in the back if he held straight on for
Bridger.

The thing that messed up his plan was that Raider
had decided to pull off the road here for lunch.

Raider shuddered. If it hadn't been for his belly's
bitching—

The point was, he had turned off the road. The
gunman fired before he wanted to. It was either that or
stand around hoping Raider never got curious enough to
do any sightseeing inside the old relay station barn or
wanted to step in there to take a crap or whatever. So
the guy changed his plan at the last moment and fired
before he really wanted to. Probably the thump Raider
heard when he turned off the road was the ambusher
rushing back from the north window to the south and
knocking a board over or whatever.

Raider shook his head. All of this was real interesting, he decided. But why the hell was somebody trying
to cut him down to begin with? And who could have
known that Raider was going to be riding in this direction? Those were things he intended to find out.

He went back out to the dun and rummaged inside
his saddlebags for his spare cartridges. The way things
were going lately he didn't think he wanted to get
caught short.

The food he'd bought down the way was in there too
but he didn't feel so hungry now.

One thing he knew for sure. From here on he intended to ride with his feet loose in the stirrups and his
butt light on the saddle. Whoever the guy was, he
couldn't stay unlucky forever. And from here on out
Raider didn't intend to let luck play a part in things.

CHAPTER TWENTY

Raider wasn't a hundred percent positive he knew which way Violet and Les Thorn had headed from the intersection, but he had a hunch he could find out easily enough.

Instead of looking for wagon tracks on either road, which could have been left by any wagon and might have nothing to do with the Thorns, he went in the direction the ambusher had fled and invested an hour in sorting through the rocks and gravel until he had a good idea of where the rifleman was going. Which turned out to be the Uintas, not Evanston or Fort Bridger. The man with the .44-40 was by now somewhere ahead of him on the old cutoff to the Uinta Mountains.

Raider's reasoning was simple, if as yet unproven. He was trying to locate Violet Sigmond Thorn. And twice now someone had attempted to gun him down while he was busy doing that. It strained coincidence beyond the breaking point to think that the ambush attempts were not connected. He couldn't for the life of him figure out why anyone would give a fat crap if he told Violet her dad was dead and she was in line for an inheritance.

He drew the dun to a halt, eyes searching the country ahead for any sign of another ambush attempt. He was on open ground here, the nearest tree line three quarters

of a mile or so distant. No one was going to try a
.44-40 shot at that range. And if anyone did, Raider
could safely stand and laugh at the dumb son of a bitch.
A .44-40 is a hard hitting cartridge, its slugs heavy and
flat-nosed and carrying a helluva wallop. But the things
had a trajectory like a rainbow, and it took a steady
hand and a close-held aim to hit a target the size of a
man at anything more than two hundred yards with one.
A *real* steady hand and a damn well crafted gun barrel.
The ambusher's original idea of not risking his shot
until Raider's back was within forty yards was realistic
for an average marksman wanting to be sure of his shot.
A mediocre marksman had just about the same dead
certain range with a carbine that Raider or any other
excellent sharpshooter would have with a revolver. And
Raider's impression to this point was that the ambusher
he was dealing with here was no kind of superior
gunfighter, just an ordinary guy with a yen for Raider's
scalp and reasons of his own for wanting it.

Before Raider dismounted and made a cold lunch out
of his saddlebag provisions, he checked the surrounding
area carefully to be sure there was nothing anywhere
nearby behind which anybody could hide. Raider remembered that in Arizona and New Mexico Territories
there were some Apaches who made a pretty good
living by setting ambushes where it was clearly impossible for there to be one. He figured a little extra
caution wasn't unreasonable at this point.

Raider stripped the bridle off the dun and hobbled it
so it could graze while he hunkered without a fire to
chew on some dried beef and do some thinking.

Something was going on here that he didn't know
about. That was plain right on the face of things.
Otherwise folks with shotguns and rifles wouldn't be
wanting to perforate him in a permanent way.

Just moments ago he'd sat there on that saddle thinking there shouldn't be any reason why anybody would
want Roy Sigmond's sister to remain ignorant of her

inheritance. Maybe, just maybe, Raider was wrong about that.

Back in Omaha Sigmond had been concerned with getting Raider to find Violet for him. He'd been real specific about Violet and where he thought Raider should start looking for her and what she looked like and all that, but the man hadn't gone into any detail about the Sigmond family.

Hell, he obviously hadn't thought there was any need for that. No quarrel. Raider hadn't thought so himself. Sigmond had been right there in front of him. He could've asked if he'd wanted. But Sigmond didn't volunteer any small talk about the home folks, and Raider hadn't seen any reason to ask.

So what if—just what if—there were other boys and girls in the Sigmond clan?

What happened to Violet's inheritance if Roy—that is, the Pinkerton Detective Agency acting on Roy's behalf— wasn't able to find the missing heiress?

A brother or several might participate in the divvying up? Or a sister? Or for that matter, Roy's stunner of a wife Eleanor?

Eleanor was fine to look at, but she also seemed the kind of thoroughbred that'd be expensive to maintain. What if she or maybe some unmentioned brother or sister thought there wasn't enough to go around if Violet got hers? That would certainly explain the strange shit that was going on with this seemingly simple missing persons case. Keep Violet out of the picture, and there would be bigger remaining slices of the Sigmond inheritance pie for those who did get a share.

Roy and Eleanor, for instance. Raider *knew* Eleanor existed. The possibility of others in the family he was guessing at. But he knew about Eleanor. And he knew as well, of course, that Eleanor was damn well aware of the search for Violet because Roy's wife had been right there in the room with them when they were discussing it in Omaha. So put Eleanor at the top of the list of suspects, but keep room open at the bottom for any brothers or sisters he might learn about.

Raider grunted and plucked a grass stem to chew on while he hunkered there in the early afternoon sunlight. The juice of the green grass was faintly sweet on his tongue. He shifted the stem from one side of his mouth to the other and frowned as he tried to work this notion through.

The simple and obvious thing was to step up and ask Roy. Sure. Hey, Roy. D'you have any brothers or sisters an' if you do, might one or all of 'em be tryin' t' blow my head off?

Raider shook his as yet intact head and spit the thoroughly chewed grass stem onto the ground between his feet. That approach wouldn't do for several reasons. One of them was that Roy Sigmond, like anybody else, wouldn't be about to believe that his very own kin could be involved in attempted murder. Just the simple fact of asking was apt to get Roy's back up. Likely make him pissed off and defensive and no help at all in getting honest answers to what was basically a damned insulting question about a man's kinfolk.

Second and much more important, though, if it was Eleanor who was behind the shootings, any question put to Roy would tip her off that Raider was suspicious. He had the impression from that little session in Omaha that anything that went into Roy's ear shot right straight through and on into Eleanor's.

Raider damn sure didn't want to do anything that could spook his prime suspect.

He pondered that for a moment, then smiled. Hell, it was about time Pinkerton did something to help, anyway. Let the boys in Chicago do some nosing around on Raider's behalf. Raider grunted softly into the silence of this big, wide open country. He'd fire off a telegram to Chicago next time he reached the wires. And another, innocent one to Sigmond back in Salt Lake City letting Roy know the agency was still on the job. No way to know for sure now, Raider realized, but the information just might come in handy. And he wouldn't know one way or the other until he heard back from the Agency.

That decision reached, Raider stood and stretched and headed toward the grazing dun.

This was likely to be a long and difficult ride ahead since he wanted to follow the old road without making a target of himself while he was doing it.

He hoped, though, that Violet and Les were up ahead just a ways. And once she was located and the inheritance safely collected, it wouldn't matter worth a damn what Eleanor Sigmond or any brothers and sisters might think or want on the subject. What he could do after he found her, Raider decided, was trail along with her until the thing was settled and she wouldn't be in any possible danger.

He slipped the bridle back onto the dun and swung into the saddle for a long and, he hoped, a boring ride to the next telegraph office.

CHAPTER TWENTY-ONE

The town was called Creel City. Though calling it a city seemed a bit optimistic. It was barely big enough to be considered a village. Raider reached it without incident but not without some degree of difficulty. He'd followed the road by paralleling it, not riding on it, staying south of the grade a half mile or more.

The only person he'd seen along the way was a man sitting in a nest of rocks overlooking the road. That was in a thin string of low hills a dozen miles west of Creel City. Raider never did get a good look at the man. All he saw of the fellow was his hat and shoulders and those from a distance of more than a half mile. The man could have been his persistent ambusher, or he might as easily have been a sheepherder having lunch. In any case he was in a position that could be defended easily and effectively if he decided to get hostile, and Raider rode wide of him without ever being seen.

Creel City was a farming community located on a broad plain with a thread of water running through after spilling out of the Uinta Mountains to the east.

Somewhere up in those mountains was Silver Canyon and the Sigmond holdings.

With any kind of luck— Raider shook his head, impatient with himself. Luck wasn't what cut it.

He located the telegraph office but didn't enter it

right away. He needed some time to encode his message to Chicago. The way things were going lately he decided it would be better to handle it that way than to send a wire that could be read in plain English. Instead he found a café.

The choice of where to eat was an easy one. There was only one eatery in Creel City. Small as the place was—and empty at this late afternoon time of day— it was being run by three young women. Three people to wait on six tables. Oughta be damn good service, he decided.

He chose a seat in the back corner where his back was to walls in both directions and gave the waitress a smile.

She gave him a suspicious scowl in return. "We have stew, coffee, and bread. No pie. That won't be ready till supper."

"I think I'll have stew an' bread an' coffee," Raider said. He tried the smile again. "An' I thank you."

The young woman sniffed and walked away without acknowledging the order.

She wasn't a bad looking filly. And she had a hell of a good frown. Plenty of practice, he decided.

Raider rummaged in his saddlebags for the current code book, licked the point of the pencil stub he'd somehow managed to avoid losing, and bent over the slow, laborious task of putting what he wanted to say into incomprehensible crap, at least to anyone else's eyes.

Later, filled but not particularly pleased by a dull meal, he walked back over to the telegraph office in time to get there shortly before the posted closing hour.

The telegrapher gave him a blank look—no smile— and accepted the message Raider handed him.

"Awful long," he said.

"You got a limit these days?"

The telegrapher's response was a glance of sharp

rebuke. "Late in the day. Long message. I don't know I'll be able to get it out this afternoon."

Raider smiled at him. "I'm sure you can manage it."

The telegrapher sniffed. Kind of like that waitress had. Must be some kind of collective habit popular with the good folks of Creel City, Raider decided.

"I don't know. Long message, late in the day. And it don't make no sense. Harder to send when it don't make no sense. Can't anticipate what's coming. Man like you, doesn't know anything about the telegraph, you wouldn't understand that." He shook his head. "Nope. Don't expect I could get that out till morning."

Raider's smile didn't change a lick as he straightened to his full height, looming over the telegrapher across the small counter that separated them. He reached out and very gently tightened and reset the knot in the man's tie, then gave the operator a gentle pat on the cheek.

"Now," he said softly. There could be no mistaking the quiet menace in his voice, even though he was still smiling.

The telegrapher paled, thought about protesting, and apparently decided that wouldn't be one of his better ideas. "Yes, uh, um, I just might be able to manage it now at that."

Raider beamed his approval and appreciation. "Thanks."

The telegraph operator—he seemed to've become suddenly warm in the office because he was sweating—coughed and tugged at his necktie, then picked up the message form and carried it to the desk where the electrified key was bolted in place.

"An' just so you'll know," Raider added, "I can send an' read a key prob'ly good as you can."

"Uh, yes, sir. I intended no—"

" 'Course you didn't," Raider agreed pleasantly.

"Yes, sir. Thank you, sir." The operator opened the circuit with a quick, staccato tapping on the black sender, pushed his sleeve garters higher on his arm and bent to the genuinely slow and difficult job of transmitting a coded message.

Raider leaned comfortably on the counter behind him every moment of the time it took, smiling all the while and looking just as pleasant as could be.

CHAPTER TWENTY-TWO

Strange damn town, Raider thought. It seemed to be full of dour men of all ages and descriptions and long-faced women who were mostly in their thirties or younger. There wasn't a smile or a nod or a howdy in the lot of them.

After the coded telegraph message was successfully—and accurately—transmitted to Chicago, Raider walked down the block to one of the two general mercantile stores in Creel City and was lucky enough to find the place still open. Like the café in the next block, the mercantile was run by women, in this case by a pair of women somewhere in their twenties who almost had to be sisters. They both had strawberry hair, sunken cheeks, and no figure to speak of. They weren't twins, though. Raider guessed there would be two, three years between them.

"Ladies." He smiled and touched the brim of his Stetson.

He got back looks with less welcome and interest than you'd see in a cow's eyes at a feedlot.

He tried again. "I was hoping to buy some provisions, ladies."

The younger sister glanced at the older one; the older one pointed toward a line of shelving on a side wall.

"Thank you very much for all your assistance," Raider said. He was damn well proud of himself. He was able to keep every last hint of sarcasm out of his voice when he said it.

He wandered over to the indicated shelves and took his time looking over the offerings. They weren't all that diversified, but there was enough a man could get by on. He pulled down a can of this and a poke of that and piled everything onto a nearby stack of brown canvas overalls that felt stiff and heavy enough to turn bullets. Hell, maybe he should buy a pair and quit worrying about that damned ambusher. When his selections were complete he gathered them into both arms and carried them to the counter at the back of the little store.

Neither sister had moved an eyelash the whole time. Now the older sister glanced down at Raider's purchases and gave them a very brief inspection.

Gotcha, he thought. Now at least one of them would have to say something.

"Two dollars," the older one said. She might have become a sour old biddy before her time, but her voice was actually quite nice. If she ever learned to smile she wouldn't be half bad.

It occurred to him that she hadn't bothered to tote up an amount item by item or even really look to see what all he was buying. And there might be a dollar's worth of stuff on the counter there, if the prices were high hereabouts.

He suspected, though, that the choice was clearly his. He could either pay her the two dollars or go down the street to the competing mercantile. With his luck in Creel City that store would likely be closed by now.

He paid the two bucks.

"Thank you very much, ladies."

Neither of them moved. Move? Shit, they didn't blink.

"Could I have a sack for this stuff, please?"

The younger one turned around—hell of a lot of activity and excitement, everything considered—picked up a burlap sack off a pile of them, and handed it to him. She handled the bag with just the tips of two fingers. No chance of her touching his hand that way. Good idea, he decided. A body just never knew what kind of contamination a stranger could pass along. Hell, in a backward little pisshole like this she might be scared she'd get knocked up if their fingers touched.

"Very kind o' you. Thanks." Raider dropped the cans and other things into the bag and touched the brim of his hat with a big, happy smile.

Yessirree, boy. This here Creel City was dandy. Guy might yearn to come here an' live when he retired, just for the atmosphere and friendliness.

He carried the bag out to the dun and tied it securely behind his cantle, then looked around.

All this nonstop talkativeness was making him thirsty.

People passing on the street, he noticed, walked by without a look in his direction. Not a lick of curiosity in the crowd, apparently. And strangers couldn't be all that common in Creel City, Utah.

He didn't see any signs for saloons anywhere on the lone street of the business district. Maybe somewhere out at the edge of town? He could believe just about anything here, including or even especially a straitlaced desire to interfere in everybody else's pleasures.

He mounted the dun and rode out to one end of town, then turned around and rode back to have a look at the other.

He found a dilapidated shed, an abandoned well, and a couple bare foundations where buildings used to stand.

But no saloon.

As far as Raider could determine, there wasn't a place anywhere in or near Creel City where a man could buy himself a drink.

He smiled a little. Hell, maybe he'd just discovered the reason everybody in this place was so glum.

On his second ride through the length of the business street he pulled the dun to a halt and damn near reached for his Remington.

Standing on the boardwalk in front of the mercantile where Raider'd just bought his groceries were three men. Two of the men were middle-aged and bearded. The third looked an awful lot like the glimpse Raider'd had of that ambusher. At least the shirt color seemed right. And the man was standing now with his back to Raider, which was the same view he'd had of the rifleman this morning.

One of the men with the beards and big bellies said something to the other two and all three of them swiveled their heads to give Raider a stare.

The guy who might—or might not—be Raider's faithful follower had the exact same blank look on him that everybody else in this jerkwater burg wore as a matter of habit.

A local boy, Raider decided with a frown. A definite Creel City resident. He damn sure wasn't any stranger here or those two wouldn't be talking with him so thick. The posture of all three of them said they were easy with each other if not particularly demonstrative about it. And the guy who wanted to make Raider quit breathing was a Salt Lake product. Not Creel City.

Until Raider rode in this afternoon and spotted the fading sign posted along the road he hadn't ever known there was such a place as Creel City. So this local boy wasn't the man Raider thought he was. The shirt was similar but apparently that's as far as it went.

Raider nodded to the three men on the sidewalk and rode the dun to the far end of town again.

He couldn't find a drink here, but he could set up camp near the tumble-down shed and get ready for an early start in the morning. With luck there would still be water in the well down that way and Raider wouldn't have to bother anyone in town for some or trust to the quality of the surface water in the creek just east of town.

He suspected he wasn't going to be all that unhappy to ride away from Creel City in the morning. In fact, the earlier the better.

CHAPTER TWENTY-THREE

Raider woke with a sense that something was wrong. That there was some unknown thing awry in the night although he could recall having heard no sound or movement to bring him from deep sleep into an instant awareness of his surroundings.

He had been asleep, he guessed, less than an hour. The wheel of the stars rotating slowly overhead told him that much.

Nearby the dun horse was contentedly cropping grass at the end of its picket and tether.

Raider rolled quietly onto his belly and slipped the Remington free of the holster.

He was watching the side of the shed some thirty yards away. Earlier he had built a fire there, cooked and ate a leisurely meal, and made a show of bedding down under the shelter of what remained of the shed roof. As soon as the firelight died, though, he silently moved outside. Anyone interested enough to keep a watch on him would think he was still inside the shed.

There was little light in the moonless sky, but the faint glow of starlight was enough for eyes thoroughly accustomed to the dark.

Off to his right the town of Creel City was as silent and still as the night itself. No nightlife here. No honky-

tonks or saloons or rowdiness. The sun was down and
so were the residents of the town.

Raider did not try to keep a watch on all the shifting
shadows around the remains of the small shed. Instead
he watched the dun horse, nicely silhouetted for him
against the starlit sky from Raider's position on the
ground at hoof level.

The horse tore a mouthful of grass free with a sound
that seemed loud in the stillness. He could hear its teeth
as it ground the grass stems into a pulp, then extend its
neck toward another clump. The dun took a half step
forward, stopped, and raised its head. Its ears were
erect. One ear twitched, and then both ears swiveled
and pointed. It raised its muzzle as if testing what little
breeze there was but did not whinny.

Raider smiled grimly to himself. Someone was approaching the shed. And doing it very quietly.

The horse's pointing ears showed him precisely where
to look in the shadows. He spotted the figure then.
Motionless, then creeping slowly on. A cloud drifting
silently far overhead moved past, and the starlight showed
him a human form hunched low to the ground. Oddly,
the person seemed to be paying more attention to the
dark bulk of the town buildings than to the shed.

Raider frowned. A gunman, one would think, should
be more intent on the quarry than the background. He
held the Remington ready but did not cock it. There was
something—

"Pssst. Mister. Mister Pinkerton man."

The whisper was soft on the night air. And feminine.

Raider sat upright, the blanket he'd been wrapped in
dropping off his shoulders unheeded.

"Mister," the whisper repeated.

She was approaching the shed now. As soon as the
weathered, sagging frame of the old structure was between her and the town she stood upright and moved
more quickly.

Raider rose to his feet and ghosted forward in sock

feet. He moved without noise to a point not three feet behind her shoulder without her ever knowing he was there. Her attention was on the floor inside the shed. She acted like she wanted to waken but not startle him.

"Pssst. Mister. Please?"

"Here," Raider said softly.

She jumped damn near out of her skin, but she made no noise. She didn't shout or scream as he'd more than half expected her to do.

"M'gosh, mister." She turned to face him, one hand pressed over a trembling, meager breast. "You didn' have to do that."

Raider recognized her now. She was the younger sister from the mercantile where he'd stopped for provisions this evening.

He laid a finger to his lips, although she certainly gave no indication that she wanted noise any more than he did, and drew her back to the patch of brush where he'd made his bed for the night. She came with him without objection and obeyed the tug of his hand that pulled her down to the ground. Both of them sat on Raider's blanket and ground cloth. He didn't want to make a target of himself any more now than he had earlier.

"I take it you wanted t' see me?" His voice was very low. The sound of it wouldn't carry more than a few feet.

The girl nervously eyed his lap, and he realized he was still holding the big revolver with the muzzle casually directed more or less toward her stomach. "Sorry." He slid the heavy weapon back into the holster.

"Thank you." He could see the set of her shoulders relax.

He nodded.

"You're the man from Pinkerton's aren't you?" she asked.

Raider shrugged. Obviously—because of that telegraph operator, he guessed—the people here already knew about him. There seemed no need to give anything away though.

"You got to leave, mister," the girl said with a low, intense urgency. She leaned forward and touched his wrist to emphasize the warning. "Please. We—you don't know. There's things you don't understand, mister. We don't want no trouble. You got to leave. Just—leave us be. Please." Her voice had risen in volume as she spoke, forgetting the need for quiet. ·

"Shhh."

She stopped and gave him a puzzled look. Then seemed to realize. When she spoke again it was once more in a low whisper. "All we want is to be let be, mister. To do what's right. You know?"

As a matter of fact, he didn't know. He had no idea what in hell this girl was talking about.

"Just leave us be, mister. There's been troubles enough over this."

"Over what?"

That simple but basic question seemed to take her aback. She hesitated and gave him a close, searching look as if she were trying to decide if he was serious or not.

"Look, dammit," he whispered back at her, "I didn't come here t' cause trouble for nobody in Creel City. Jeez, lady, I never heard o' the place till I come inta the town limits this afternoon. I don't know what you folks think I'm doin' here, but all it is, is passin' through. So what is it you're all scared of 'round here that the sight of a Pink would make y' all so crazy nervous?"

"Oh, dear," the girl said. The hand that had been on her trembling breast earlier jumped now to her mouth. "You don't mean to tell me— You aren't chasing after sweet Violet?"

Sweet Violet? These people did have something to do with the Thorns, then. But what? And why?

Before Raider could decide how, or if, to answer her the girl stood, exposing herself in the starlight. She turned toward the shadows near the town buildings and waved her arms.

"Don't—" Raider started to say.

"Don't—" the girl started to shout.

A lance of painfully bright yellow flame spat out of the darkness, followed an instant later by the ear-numbing report of a gunshot.

Raider grabbed the girl around the waist and tried to sweep her down to the comparative safety of ground level, but he knew already that he was too late. He could feel the taut, sudden tension in her slim body as she twisted under the impact of the bullet. She gasped and went limp in his arms.

Raider could hear footsteps pound as the shooter tried to get away.

Even as the girl's body was falling in his arms he was trying to pull away. Trying to get to the Remington that lay in its holster on his blanket. The dying girl's weight came down on his right shoulder and impeded his draw. By the time Raider could free himself of her and get to his gun the footsteps were gone.

And in the distant night there were no lamps lighted, no voices raised. Creel City lay dark and silent as if soundly, peacefully asleep.

"Son of a bitch," Raider muttered. He belted his holster around his hips and dropped the big Remington into it.

By the time he leaned low over the girl's form she was gone. He bent close to her lips, but there was no breath to be felt there, and her scrawny breast would tremble no more.

He crouched in the darkness over her. Logically, and normally, the proper thing to do would be to raise an alarm and light lanterns and find the authorities to report the shooting to.

But that would be the normal thing to do. There wasn't a whole lot about Creel City, Utah, that was normal.

The girl had been warning him to leave. She didn't

want him shot? Perhaps she knew another ambush was in the works and didn't want guilty knowledge on her conscience? Probably. Although Raider was unlikely to ever know the answers for certain.

The whole town was fomenting against the presence of a Pinkerton operative here. The dead girl had as good as said so. And the town was against him because of Violet Thorn. She had said that too. But why? And how would they know it was Violet that Raider wanted to find? They were questions he wished he could ask. But he couldn't expect any help from anyone in Creel City. And he damn sure couldn't ask the girl who'd come to warn him away from the danger that instead claimed her.

"There's been troubles enough over this." That's what she had said. Raider could play the words back in his mind and recall the exact tone of her voice when she spoke them.

There's been troubles enough over this. What troubles? Over what, damn it? What the hell was going on here?

Raider knelt beside the dead girl's body and reached a decision that he hated to make but which seemed inescapable. There was nothing he could do now for this dead girl whose name he did not even know. And he did not want to start a gunfight with the entire population of Creel City, Utah. He knelt there glaring toward the blank, darkened windows of the stores and houses of Creel City. Still no one had come outside to investigate the gunshot nor to inquire after the girl who had shouted in the night.

For whatever reasons, these people did not want him to find Violet Thorn, did not want Violet to receive her inheritance. Why a whole, crazy town would care about that, Raider could not comprehend. But maybe, just maybe, he could do something about it. If first he found Violet Thorn and secured for her her future and her husband's. Then he just might be able to come back here and get something straight with these sons of bitches.

He very carefully straightened the dead girl's limbs and arranged her hands over her stomach. He tugged the hem of her dress down where it belonged and pressed her sightless eyes closed with the palm of his hand. There was nothing more he could do for this girl who had wanted to save his life. Yet.

Raider gathered his things together and carried them to the side of the nervous dun horse.

CHAPTER TWENTY-FOUR

The road forked. Raider had climbed onto the first gentle slope of the Uintas, following the same road he was sure Les and Violet Thorn had taken after they left Salt Lake City. But now the road split, and he had no idea which leg went toward Silver Canyon. From here both branches angled and wound into the mountains, but there were no signs posted. And the last humans he'd seen that he might have asked were back in Creel City.

By now those crazy bastards were probably looking for him on a charge of murder. It seemed unlikely that anyone would have stepped forward and volunteered the information that it was he, and not the Pinkerton, who had shot the girl whose body they would've found come daylight. So, no, it didn't seem like a particularly good idea to turn around and ride seven hours back in that direction to find out which road to take here.

Raider dismounted and loosened his cinches so the dun could relax and graze while he tried to work out the more likely direction to take for Silver Canyon. The horse hadn't been used hard but it had been used steadily through the night after Raider pulled quietly out of Creel City, and it was probably needing the rest. Particularly since from here on the road was likely to be uphill, whichever way he chose. From what Raider could see from here, the two road branches both climbed considerably, one heading generally north and the other south. All he knew about Roy Sigmond's home town was that it was somewhere in the Uintas. North, south— toss a coin.

Raider pulled a can of pickled beef out of the burlap sack of provisions he'd bought back in the crazy town and ate it while the dun rested.

He left the animal saddled, though. Around here it seemed like a man just never knew when he was going to want to move along in a hurry.

The canned meat was about as tasty as one could expect. Which was on a slightly lower order than the flavor of wallpaper paste. But the stuff was filling and it didn't have to be cooked. It probably wouldn't be a good idea to show smoke and draw pictures for anybody about where he was right now. So far there'd been no sign of a posse or a still persisting ambusher behind him, but that didn't mean there was no chance that someone could be back there and just be too far away for Raider to spot him yet. He was riding with a damned careful eye on his back trail.

He ate and gave the dun a half hour to fill its own belly and pulled the cinches tight again.

When he set out again he took the left-hand fork. No good reason. Good reason? Hell, he didn't have any reason. One fork seemed as good as the other. And where there was a road, there had to be a reason for that road. Somewhere up ahead he would find people, and then he could get his bearings.

He set the dun into a swift, steady walk that it could manage for miles on the uphill stretch.

CHAPTER TWENTY-FIVE

The community was even smaller and less imposing than Creel City, although that would have seemed hardly possible. It was a meager collection of log structures built at the mouth of a narrow gulch, the surrounding hillsides dark with fir and spruce and scattered aspen trees.

If the place had a name Raider didn't know what it was, because there was no welcome sign posted along the road and the only sign he could see on any of the few buildings was one that said "Store." Man, these folks were informative.

He drew rein outside the store and stepped off the dun. It was little past midday, but he was tired. He'd been in the saddle all of yesterday and most of last night and twice someone had tried to kill him. All in all somewhat wearying.

A man came to the open front door of the store as Raider dismounted. He was wearing an apron that once had been white, and his hands were tucked behind the bib of the thing as if he were resting them there.

Raider smiled grimly. There was something in the rigid tenseness of the man's right arm—and something more in his eyes—that suggested there was more beneath the bib of that apron than eight fingers and two thumbs. Something small and deadly perhaps? Raider was in no mood to play games or to have any played with him.

"Mister, which would you ruther. You wanta bring them hands out where I can see 'em or d' you wanta try me? Personally, I don't give a shit which, but I'd 'preciate it if you'd make up your mind quick."

The storekeeper flushed a dark red and quickly snatched his hands out from under the apron. He gave Raider a look of close appraisal, then nodded. "You vould be de man from Chick-ago. Velcome." His accent was thick. German, Slav, something like that, Raider guessed. Raider didn't look down on him for it. Hell, this guy spoke pretty good English. And a lot better German or Slav or whatever than Raider ever would. A man who could put a loop over more than one language had to have something between his ears.

Interesting, though, how in this jerkwater collection of shanties not even big enough to be a village the Pinkerton man was also expected. And this time there wasn't any telegraph operator to pass the word along.

Raider paid some attention to the empty doors and windows of the buildings behind him. If he got the same kind of reception here that he had in Creel City—

"Come." It sounded more like "koom" the way the storekeeper said it.

"You wouldn't mind shucking the artillery first, would you?"

The man cocked his head and seemed to think that over for a moment, probably trying to translate the idiomatic English into something he could cope with, then smiled and nodded. "Ach. I do." He reached very carefully under the apron bib with his left hand and extracted a shiny little four-barrel Sharps Ace that he cheerfully showed to Raider and then dropped into the deep left-hand pocket of his trousers. The little gun couldn't be any danger down there unless you gave the guy a five minute head start on getting it out. "Now you koom?"

"Now I koom," Raider agreed. He followed the man inside the low-roofed log store.

The inside of the place was dark and cool. It was filled with mouth-watering smells from smoked hams and bacon hanging from the low rafters and the sharper, spicier aroma of the brine in an open pickle barrel near the counter.

No wonder the place was just called "Store." There wouldn't have been any other reasonable way to describe all the things the store sold. It passed a general mercantile's offerings by a mile in variety if not necessarily in quantity. There seemed to be at least one of everything lodged under that one none too large roof, most of it stacked in piles all over the dirt floor.

"De man from Chick-ago iss heer," the storekeeper announced. Then he added something else in a guttural tongue.

Raider decided he was glad the people inside the store weren't as hostile as those back in Creel City—or at least hadn't demonstrated the fact yet if it turned out they were—because it took him several long, unnerving seconds for his eyes to adjust to the gloom indoors after the bright sunshine on the other side of the logs.

It turned out there were three men seated on three-legged stools near a greased and blackened stove that had been cleaned for the summer's disuse but that still seemed to be the focal point of gatherings in the store.

All of them were younger than the keeper of the store, but otherwise all of them looked remarkably like him. Their features were individual enough, but all four men wore thick, spade beards and black coats and shirts buttoned high but worn without ties or collars. Raider wondered for a moment if he'd blundered into a colony of Amish way the hell and gone in the middle of the Uintas. They spoke a sort of German. Then he reconsidered. As far as he could recall, the Amish were pacifists who didn't go around carrying hideout weapons under their aprons.

He could see a curved, parrot-beak revolver grip sticking out of one of the seated men's waistbands, and there were a bunch of heavy caliber rifles stacked against the wall behind the cold stove too. Cheap but lethal government surplus .50-70 Springfields, they looked like. The old trapdoor conversion Springfield was a rifle a man could buy for a buck and half and make a fortune with slaughtering buffalo. If a man could find a herd of buffalo, that is.

Raider nodded to the welcome party and strolled over to lean against the counter where his back was to a wall and he could keep the entire crowded room in view.

"Gentlemen." He nodded to them.

The three gave him a looking over, then turned their faces toward the center of their circle and rattled and coughed something off in one of the many languages Raider hadn't any knowledge of. They spoke among themselves for a moment and then turned back to him, all smiles and pleasantry. One by one they came forward, gave him a stiff little bow and offered a hand for him to shake. When Raider'd done that each of the three of them bowed to him again, went back to the stove long enough to pick up a Springfield rifle and walked out of the place.

Strange.

If these guys knew who he was—maybe he should feel flattered to be recognized in places where he hadn't even known there were places until five minutes ago— they probably knew why he was here too.

But what in hell was going on around here?

"Have the Thorns passed through here?" he asked the keeper of the store.

"Here? No. Never." The man's tone suggested that Raider had just asked an awfully stupid question. "Not here."

"Is this the road to Silver Canyon?"

Again the storekeeper gave him a look like maybe Raider was daft. "But of course. Yes. You don' know?"

Raider decided against pointing out the obvious and didn't answer.

"You look"—he had to search a moment for the word he wanted—"toad."

Toad? Raider sorted through a few possibilities. Toad. Towed? Hell, yes. "Tired?" he suggested.

The storekeeper smiled. "Tired. Yes. Dank." He bobbed his head. "You eat. Rest. Ve talk later, yes?"

Raider wasn't a hundred percent sure about this arrangement yet. But he could use a good meal and a few hours of sleep. He nodded. "If you have someplace, uh, private?"

The storekeeper grinned. "Safe. Yes. I show you. Koom."

When they went back outside Raider saw that the dun horse had already been taken away and presumably tended to while he was indoors. Either that or these oddballs were up to something sneakier than Raider could figure out right now.

The hell with it. He wanted some sleep, and so far it looked like these folks wanted to make that available to him.

He allowed himself to be escorted to the very welcome hospitality of a sturdy log cabin built with its back against solid rock. And with a very sturdy bar across the only door in or out. His gear was already laid out in there waiting for him. And something more in the way of hospitality too. *Real* hospitality.

He smiled to the blonde and buxom young woman who rose off the side of the bunk as he came in.

"Hello."

CHAPTER TWENTY-SIX

Whatever the girl said, it wasn't hello, or anything else he recognized.

But there wasn't a hell of a lot of doubt about why she was there. She was an accommodation of sorts. Available if he wished to use her. Surely this wasn't the way quite everybody was greeted around here. Or hell, maybe it was. This whole end of Utah seemed to be filled with people who were nuts anyway. Maybe this was considered normal hospitality in the Uintas. Criminy!

Of course the fact was that the men at the store knew he was a Pinkerton operative. They couldn't have been expecting him, but they'd sure been told about him. So really this was likely their idea of being helpful. Very helpful indeed, Raider decided.

He turned to ask the English-speaking storekeeper about it, but the man had walked away and was already halfway back to his store. There was no sign of anybody else around. The three men who'd been sitting around the stove when Raider came in were long gone now.

Raider shrugged and turned back to face the girl. She had a plump, round face and bright red cheeks. Her blonde hair was done up in tight braids that were pinned to the sides of her head like a pair of small wheels clamped in place there. She was barefoot, he saw, and was wearing a much washed and slightly frayed plain dress of faded gray. Her sleeves were rolled up. Her hands and forearms were pink. He got the impression she spent a lot of time with her hands in water washing dishes or clothes or floors or whatever.

Not that she needed to wash the floor in this place. The floor of the cabin was packed earth that had taken on a hard crust from being soaked and smoothed through years of use.

The girl said something in the language Raider couldn't follow. He smiled at her. It seemed the thing to do.

He closed the door and carefully bolted it.

The girl motioned toward the bunk and lifted an eyebrow.

Raider grinned.

She damn sure wasn't shy. She gave him an appraising look and then a wide, happy smile as she began to unbutton the front of her dress.

Raider hadn't exactly walked in with this in mind, but it didn't take much to change the direction of his thinking.

The girl slipped the dress off her shoulders and stepped out of it as it fell in a loose heap to the dirt floor. She wasn't wearing anything under it. Not even cotton drawers.

She stood in front of him naked and proud, and her eyes invited him to look her over.

What he saw, he admitted, was nice.

She had a full figure with large breasts that still had the taut uplift of youth, wide hips, prettily dimpled knees. Her nipples were large but exceptionally pale, as was her pubic hair. At first glance she looked like she was shaved there, but that was only because her hair was so very pale as to be almost unnoticeable until closer inspection.

Raider inspected her more closely. He went to her, and she tipped her head back and smiled up at him. Her eyes were a bright, intense blue. The pink, moist tip of her tongue came out to slide slowly over full lips. She laughed and pressed herself to him, lifting her mouth to his in an invitation that was unmistakable.

Raider kissed her. He discovered that her breath was sweet. She tasted mildly of cloves and salt.

He put his arms around her and caressed her back as she pressed her pelvis against him with a soft, satisfied moan. Her mouth opened wider, and her tongue probed delicately.

He stepped back and stroked her cheek, then pointed to himself and said, "Raider."

She grinned, pointed to her own chest and said, "Erika."

"Hello, Erika."

She said something back, the only word of which he could understand was Raider. Both of them grinned.

Erika's work-roughened hands traced lightly over his chest and sides for a moment, then became busy with the task of getting him out of his clothes.

Raider didn't try to stop her.

When Raider was out of his things Erika took them and carefully folded and tidied each garment and placed them on the small table that, with the homemade bunk, comprised the primary furniture in the small, snug cabin.

Light filtered in through uncaulked chinks between the logs. The interior of the place was cool and comfortable. Particularly with Erika there.

She motioned for him to sit while she took care of his clothes. He perched on the side of the bunk and watched her. She moved nicely with a swift, efficient grace. She had, he saw, a very round, pretty ass.

When she was done he moved over against the wall to give her room to join him.

Erika sat on the bed at his side. She ran her hands lightly over his body, stopping with an admiring chuckle to fondle and play with him when she got slightly south of where his belt buckle would have been.

She hefted his balls on one palm, cupping and warming them, and gently traced the length of his very erect cock with the fingertips of her other hand.

She said something to him and smiled.

Raider laughed and returned the favor by stroking her breast. It was weighty and full, and when he rolled her nipple between his thumb and forefinger it enlarged and stiffened.

Erika giggled and gave him a playful wink.

She ducked her head and planted an entirely too swift kiss, loud and wet, on the tip of his pecker, then cheerfully pushed him down on his back while she straddled him.

"Hey, now. Shouldn't we—?"

Too late.

Erika giggled again. She pressed her hands flat on his chest and wiggled her hips. She was wet and ready and rather large.

Just that easily he felt himself sliding inside her. Very deep inside her. The heat of her enveloped and held him.

Erika sighed, and her eyes sagged nearly closed. She threw her head back and sat upright.

When she moved her hips in slow, lazy circles it was like being inside a churn of hot, fresh butter. He could feel himself shifting and rotating inside her as Erika moved on top of him. The sensation, all in all, was very nice, very warm, very soothing.

With a small grunt of effort, Erika pushed against his chest and levered herself upward while she brought her feet closer to his sides so that instead of resting her weight on Raider's pelvis she was supporting herself above him, crouching there so that once she got her balance and lifted her hands away the only contact between their bodies was at his rigid, throbbing shaft which was socketed deep inside her receptive body.

Damn, Raider thought. This wasn't half bad.

Erika gave him another wink and once again began to shift and rotate her hips.

Oh, my. Oh my, indeed.

She leaned backward, nearly lost her balance and when she recovered, reached behind her ample buttocks to find and lightly, teasingly tickle Raider's scrotum while she continued to move and pump above him.

She was so wet he thought he could feel Erika's juices trickle off the base of his cock and run down over his balls.

Her head lolled back, and he could see the tendons stand out sharp and clear on the side of her neck as her own pleasure mounted toward a bursting point. As indeed his was too.

He wasn't really ready for this to end. He thought about stopping her, but too late.

Erika stiffened and cried out. He felt the strong, muscular clench of her pussy contracting and pulsing tight around his cock as she reached a climax.

That was all he needed to send him spilling over the edge too, and with a convulsive upward lunge of his hips he spewed hot, sticky fluids deep inside her. The pleasure continued in short, intense jets over a period of long, exhausting seconds until finally Raider fell back against the bunk in limp relief.

Erika had stayed with him the whole while, milking and draining him completely. Now, though, she permitted herself to relax too. She dropped to the surface of the bunk with her knees tight against his sides and leaned forward until her weight was taken on his chest and pelvis. Her body was warm and damp and comfortable there.

Raider tried to say something, but Erika stopped him with a contented smile and a kiss.

She closed her eyes and pressed her face against the side of Raider's neck. A moment later he could feel in the slow, deep rhythm of her breathing that she had drifted almost instantly into sleep.

What the hell, he thought. Wouldn't be polite to disturb her now. He moved a little to take her weight more comfortably atop him and closed his eyes. A nap would be nice right now, and it would be awfully convenient to wake up still inside Erika.

CHAPTER TWENTY-SEVEN

Raider woke up with a sense of urgent, unidentified alarm. Something half heard or half sensed had brought him out of his shallow sleep and into instant awareness.

Erika still was sleeping on his chest, her breath warm and slow against his skin. While they slept he had become limp and slipped out of her so that now he felt sticky and wet at his crotch. This hardly seemed the time to be worrying about that, though.

With one hand he prodded at Erika, trying to roll her off him. With the other he was reaching for the holstered Remington that should have been at his side.

Where was the—oh, shit. She'd wrapped the gunbelt tidily and carefully around the heavy holster and laid it on the table with the rest of his things. It had happened so naturally that he hadn't even thought about it. With a heart-leaping surge of sudden concern he shoved Erika rudely aside and lurched off the bed to grab for the revolver on the table. By the time he had a moment to think and to analyze the situation he was standing bare-assed in the middle of the dirt floor with the gun cocked and aimed at the cabin door.

Erika was behind him crying now and babbling something in the language he did not know.

"Hush," he told her none too gently. "Just be quiet."

The words would have meant nothing to her but

apparently the tone of voice did. She hushed and drew herself into a tight ball in the far corner of the bunk with a sheet drawn up over her breasts as if that would somehow protect her from whatever was going on here. She looked confused and frightened but damn sure no longer asleep. She started to say something.

"Shhh," Raider commanded.

He was no longer so tense. No longer crouched ready to take on a battalion of crazies from Creel City. But he wasn't about to start thinking that he had wakened like that for nothing. Something had set him off. He cocked his head and concentrated on listening. He couldn't see anything that was happening outside the cabin, but he could damn sure try to hear.

He couldn't hear a thing. Not even the sound of a breeze rustling pine needles.

In the dim light inside the cabin he could not even be sure what time it was, although it seemed that he must have slept several hours or more. Probably it was late afternoon or early evening.

He reached for his trousers. Whatever it was that woke him—

There. And again. A dull, booming report reached him. But from very far away. There had been two gunshots, a pause and then a third. There must have been a fourth shot—a first one, really—that brought him out of his sleep. It sounded like rifle fire. From behind the thick log walls of the cabin it was hard to judge how far away the fight must be. A half mile, he guessed. Possibly more.

There was another isolated shot and then a brisk, rattling volley of fire that sounded like a sheaf of twigs being snapped. The reports came too close together and too faintly to count.

"Damn," Raider muttered. He pushed the heavy Remington back into his holster and hurriedly began yanking on his clothes and boots.

Behind him Erika cowered in her corner whimpering

and afraid. That was tough, but he had no time for the accommodating blonde girl now. He had to find out what the hell was happening out there.

Somewhere nearby there was one hell of a gun battle in progress as the sound of still more fire came dull and hollow into the cabin.

Raider dressed quickly, but he did take time to strap the gunbelt in place and make sure he had spare cartridges in his pockets as well as in the gunbelt.

He stood at the door for a moment listening, the Remington again palmed and ready. He heard nothing. There seemed to be no activity anywhere near. Not even the sounds of the distant rifle shots now. Even so, when he went out it was in a low, crouching rush.

If somebody was out there—

CHAPTER TWENTY-EIGHT

Nothing greeted him but late afternoon sunlight. The bottom of the gulch where the settlement was located was in deep shadow although Raider could see daylight slanting onto the east wall of the rocky cut.

He heard one last gunshot somewhere to the south, presumably on the road he'd followed up here.

There was no sign of any of the men. Nor of anyone else for that matter. He and the girl seemed to be alone with the few buildings.

Raider had no idea where they'd taken the dun horse. And for that matter his saddle and other things were still inside the cabin with Erika. Finding the horse and saddling it would have taken more time than he wanted to waste. He ran back inside long enough to grab the Winchester out of its scabbard and then set out at a long, loping jog in the direction he'd heard the gunfire. He ran in the roadway for a quarter mile, then slipped off to the side so he would not be exposed to view from the hillsides. The settlement was located just inside the mouth of the gulch so the road was not confined by narrow walls here. The land sloped away to both sides, rising on his left and falling to the right as the road traversed the bulk of the Uintas. Raider moved into the trees on the high side and slowed to a cautious walk as he came closer to the area where the fighting must have been. The precaution was unnecessary. Another quarter mile brought him onto a hillside overlooking the public road. There were men plainly visible a hundred fifty yards away. The majority of the men Raider could see down there looked very, very dead. Of those who were still upright he recognized two of the three he'd seen at the store. Two others were unknown to him but were obviously friendly with the ones Raider believed to mean him no harm. He walked down toward them but kept the Winchester ready just in case. As he came closer he could see that the dead included the keeper of the store, no longer wearing his apron, and one of the men who'd been sitting by the cold stove when Raider went inside the place. There were five others lying bloody and twisted on the ground near them. Two of those were people Raider thought he recalled seeing back in Creel City although he wasn't entirely sure.

Whatever had happened here and for whatever reasons it had occurred, they'd had themselves a hell of a scrap. Seven dead and only four left standing.

From the looks of things, the party of Creel Cityers had been coming up the road in the open, were challenged by some of the locals moving down to block the way, and somehow the confrontation degenerated into a pretty good imitation of a small war.

Raider was well inside handgun range before any of the excited, rapidly talking survivors noticed his approach.

"Easy does it," he said.

None of them seemed interested in raising a gun toward him, though. They all appeared to recognize him, including the two Raider'd never seen before. He began to suspect that he'd ridden under their rifles on his way to the gulch and that they hadn't proved hostile. Whoever they were, he conceded, they were good at laying an ambush. He hadn't suspected their presence on his way up.

One of them, the oldest of the bunch now that the storekeeper was dead, greeted Raider calmly enough

and said something in that language that Raider wished
to hell he could fathom.

"Don't any o' you guys speak English?"

They talked that over among themselves, shrugged,
and shook their heads.

"Shit," Raider said.

One of them smiled and nodded. Raider guessed the
guy understood that much anyhow.

The man who knew what shit was smiled again and
pointed proudly toward the five dead strangers and said
something long and confusing. It sounded like he was
trying to clear his throat.

"I'm sorry. I don't know what you're tryin' t' tell
me, neighbor."

The guy shrugged and spread his palms.

"Yeah. Me too."

The four locals began stripping the dead of weapons
and ammunition. They were also prudent enough, Raider
noticed, to lift the dead men's cash. Hell, why not? It
wasn't going to do them any good to be buried with it.

Raider looked off down the road toward the south.
One of the foreigners seemed to understand what he
wanted. The guy came over to him and touched his
sleeve, then by hand motions and upraised fingers and a
makeshift semblance of sign language told him that at
least two of the Creel Cityers had gotten away from the
roadblock carnage.

"You cain't—damn, I wish you could talk English."

"Yo," the foreigner agreed. And said quite a bit
more that probably would've been helpful as hell if
Raider could just figure it out.

These guys didn't seem particularly worried about
the bodies, so Raider wasn't going to fret about them
either. The bodies of the locals were treated with careful respect while the dead Creel Cityers were tumbled
around right casual.

These people didn't like each other an awful lot,
Raider decided.

But, damn, he wished he could get some information out of these folks. Who were they? And why were they wanting to help a Pinkerton operative but blow away everybody from the nearest town? The storekeeper had said something about Violet and Lester Thorn not coming this way. "Here? No, never, not here," the guy said. Yet he said this was the road to Silver Canyon. Raider remembered that distinctly. If only because it made no damn sense. He snorted unhappily and ground a pebble into the roadbed with the heel of his boot.

All right, dammit. Violet and Lester hadn't come this way to get home to Silver Canyon. That meant they'd taken the other fork.

That, Raider supposed, was all he was likely to learn around here. It would just have to be enough. At least he knew enough now to backtrack down to the fork and ride the other leg if he wanted to catch up with the Thorns. If that was all he was going to get it was what he would just have to settle for.

Maybe the Creel Cityers and the Silver Canyon crowd got along and this bunch in the middle hated everybody? Raider grunted. But if that was so, why would both bunches be looking for a Pinkerton operative and the Creel Cityers be trying to stop him and these people wanting to be helpful? Shit, none of it made any sense. The best he could hope for at this point seemed to be finding Violet and Lester and outright asking them. And watching his back every step of the way.

He thanked the local boys for their hospitality—with Erika in mind—though he wasn't at all sure they understood any of what he was trying to tell them. Then he turned and started hiking back up toward the settlement in the gorge. It would be dusk by the time he got there, but he knew already that what he was going to do was gather up that dun horse and all his gear and get the hell out of the gulch by nightfall.

A rock mattress under a thin blanket wouldn't compare too favorably with a bunk and Erika for the night, but on the other hand Raider was more likely to wake up come morning, he figured, if he chose the less comfortable sleeping arrangement tonight.

He increased his pace and marched up the road at a brisk gait.

CHAPTER TWENTY-NINE

Raider stopped short of the fork in the seldom used road and made a cold camp in the hills overlooking the Silver Canyon leg. The foreigner back at the roadblock—funny how it was easier to think of it that way, since those men had been helpful toward him, than as the ambush that it really was—had indicated there were at least two Creel City riders somewhere ahead of Raider on this road. If the deaths of their friends had taken the fight out of them, good. If not, they would still be somewhere ahead of him and this time could be sure he would be on the other road leg if he still wanted to find Violet Thorn.

It was late, Raider reasoned. He and the dun both needed food and rest. He smiled tightly to himself. The stop in that gulch settlement had been restful in its own way. But he hadn't gotten any sleep to speak of while he was there. A couple of hours, after Erika finished wearing him down. That was all. Not that he regretted it.

He led the dun in a traverse across the slope over-looking the road and set up in a small, rock-walled nook. There was granite behind and above him, and a stand of young spruce protected him on the downslope side. Little grass grew between the trees and the rock wall, but there should be enough for one night's forage.

When he found and reclaimed the animal back at the settlement there were some leftover oat grains in the shed manger, so the foreigners probably fed the horse for him while he was otherwise occupied. He stripped the gear from the dun and put the horse on a short picket rope so it could reach what grass there was without becoming entangled in the strong, resinous spruce branches.

Then Raider took the Winchester with him and went down the slope, through the trees, so he could keep an eye on the road below without being seen. A rifle, a blanket, and a few strips of dried meat and he was set for the night. No one could come up the gravel-littered slope to reach him without him hearing their approach in plenty of time to decide if he wanted to issue an invitation or a bullet by way of greeting.

He kicked his boots off, laid the black Stetson aside and pulled the blanket over his shoulders.

This settlement looked very much like the last one except this one had a sign crudely painted and nailed to a tree proclaiming to anyone who was interested that the place was called Glory Hole.

A hole it certainly was. Glorious it was not. It lay high in the Uintas, surrounded by more rock than vegetation. Old foundations showed that once Glory Hole must have been a community of some size, if not importance, but those days were gone now. Another of the many towns and camps, Raider figured, that sprang into a brief, vigorous existence with the discovery of some precious ore, and then died almost overnight when the Glory Hole vein played out. This one seemed now to be hanging on by a thread. Fewer than a dozen log buildings showed signs they were still occupied for some purpose or other. There were two mine adit openings on the north slope above the town that looked like there might still be some desultory mining activity going on. Seven or eight other old mines were falling quickly

into ruin here, their tailings growing over with weeds
and fallen trash now.

Raider came in cautiously, the Remington loose in his
holster. A man was seated on a three-legged stool in
front of a shanty with a signboard over its door reading,
Emil Lewis, General Merchandise and Mining Supplies. He looked up from beneath the brim of his slouch
hat and didn't seem to much give a damn if anyone was
riding in or not. At least he didn't grab for a gun at the
first sight of the Pinkerton man. That was something.
Raider pulled the dun to a halt in front of him.

"Howdy."

"Howdy your own self. Something I can sell you?"
He sounded only mildly interested and not at all hopeful.

"Provisions," Raider answered. "An' maybe some
information."

The man, presumably Emil Lewis in person, mulled
that over, turned his head and spat with deadly accuracy
at the tail of a kitten playing in the dirt beside his stool.
The kitten went into a dervish whirl after its own tail in
response to the assault from an unknown quarter. The
storekeeper chuckled.

When he turned back to Raider he said. "Good profit
in selling information. You step down an' come inside,
mister. We'll see can we do business." He smiled and
stood. He was heavyset and moved slowly and clum-
sily, with a pronounced limp.

"You don't happen t' have a telegraph wire here, do
you?" Raider asked as he dismounted and tied the dun
to an eye bolt set in the front wall of the building.
There was no hitch rail provided.

"That one I'll answer free for nothing," Emil Lewis
said cheerfully. "No wires up here. You got another
thirty-five mile down the other side to reach the telegraph. Or back the way you just come."

Raider followed him inside. The interior of the store
was dark and at this elevation almost uncomfortably
cool despite bright sunshine outside.

Lewis hobbled slowly past his merchandise and eased behind a counter to sit on another, taller stool. Raider guessed he was not comfortable standing for any length of time after whatever accident or misfortune it was that robbed him of his agility.

"I'll be wantin' t' buy some supplies direc'ly, but first I'd like you t' tell me have you seen a young couple pass through here in a light wagon pulled by a mule. I got a picture here o' the lady I'm lookin' for." He dug the picture out and handed it to the man to examine.

"Ayuh. I seen this lady. Her and her husband. Come through here day before yesterday."

The Thorns were making slow time in the mountains, Raider thought, with their wagon being hauled by a single elderly mule. They had much more of a lead on him when he left Salt Lake City.

He found it interesting too that the storekeeper seemed to have no reluctance at all to give him the information.

"D' you know who I am?" Raider asked.

Emil Lewis gave him an odd look and a close inspection. "Should I? You from around here or somethin'?"

Raider smiled. "Never been here afore right this minute."

"Mister, I like guessin' games good as anybody. But somehow I don't think as how you're playin' fair if you never been here before. Me, I been here since Methuselah wore short pants. Haven't left Glory Hole since back when it deserved the name. To answer your question the short way 'round, though, no. I got no idea in hell who you are or them neither. Can't say as I care neither."

Raider relaxed. Whatever craziness it was that infected the people in Creel City and Silver Canyon, it didn't seem to have spread to Glory Hole too.

"Any other strangers pass through lately? Last night or this mornin' mebbe?" He was thinking about the Creel City rifle carriers who might still be in front of him. Just because nobody'd gotten around to shooting at him so far today didn't prove much.

"Not that I seen," the storekeeper said. "Heard something in the night that could of been horses or could of been elk. Can't say for sure which 'twas."

"You've been a big help," Raider said. He meant it. It occurred to him that he'd volunteered to pay for the information but Mr. Lewis hadn't said a word about that yet and the questions were already freely answered. Nice man. It was kind of a shame that everybody in these mountains wasn't the same way.

He selected and paid for more supplies than he really needed, food for himself and a mixture of wheat and barley for the horse, and then had to argue with the fellow when Raider offered to pay more for the purchases than Lewis had originally asked. The usual run of things, Raider reflected, was for that particular argument to work the other way, with the seller wanting more and the buyer trying to pay less. Everything being upside down and ass-backward, though, seemed about the normal order of things on this particular missing persons case. Raider guessed he should've expected it by now. He grinned and overpaid and thanked the gimpy storekeeper.

He never did get a look at any other resident of Glory Hole. Probably they were all underground trying to eke a meager living out of rock that no longer had any real riches to give up to their picks and drills. The good part of that, of course, was that no one here wanted to shoot him or seemed to give a damn that there was a Pinkerton operative in the neighborhood.

He tied the newly acquired purchases behind his cantle and remounted. Thirty-five miles, Emil Lewis had said it was, down to the next town and the telegraph wires on the east side of the Uintas. Raider would reach that, and possibly Violet Thorn too, some time the next day.

CHAPTER THIRTY

If any of the gunmen from Creel City had come this way they were conspicuous only by their absence. The ride down the other side of the Uintas might have been a Sunday jog in the park. Except, that is, for the absence of a suitable riding companion in skirts and a frilly hat. Raider wasn't going to count on a damn thing, though. He rode with his eyes open and his revolver loose in the holster, ready to jump at the first sign of anything out of place. He didn't mind the wasted caution a bit when he rode into a town that called itself Jasper without anyone shooting at him the whole way from Glory Hole. After the way things had been going lately, he felt almost like he was on vacation.

Jasper was bigger than anything he'd seen since he left Salt Lake City, although it couldn't begin to compare with that one. Certainly it was larger and more prosperous than Creel City had been. Glory Hole and the camp in the gulch, of course, weren't in the running when it came to size. He judged that Jasper probably had a population of three thousand or more.

It lay on the foothill fringes of the Uintas and the businesses that Raider could easily identify included a small smelter, a large smithy, a wheelwright's shop, and a number of general mercantiles.

Obviously Jasper serviced mining camps in the mountains, refining ore that had been reduced at local stamp mills for shipment down to the area's smelter.

The town doubled down on its future, though, by also serving ranches from the countryside around it. Raider could see a number of sheep wagons parked outside the smithy and the wheelwright's waiting for service, and where there were sheep there would probably be small scale cow operations too.

A thin thread of telegraph wire snaked across the country to the northeast. Raider figured the wire would lead eventually into Wyoming, connecting with the main line wherever it met the railroad. The coming of the telegraph to this country would've made it difficult for a man to get himself lost even if he was willing to work at it.

He pulled the dun to a halt at Jasper's livery. A taciturn hostler took the horse with a grunted comment about "two bits a day" and walked the animal off almost before Raider had time to get his gear from behind the saddle.

"An' thank you very much, neighbor," Raider said. The sarcasm was wasted, though. The hostler was already too far away to hear and obviously didn't give a damn.

Raider shouldered his bags and humped them two blocks down to the largest hotel in sight. He was working on Roy Sigmond's money. He might as well go first class.

The inside of the hotel was dark and quiet. The furnishings were massive and masculine. It was the sort of place that would cater to businessmen. Sheep and cattle buyers. Mining engineers. Too rich a place for the average traveling drummer.

"Yes, sir." The hotel clerk was polite but not over-whelmed by the privilege of being able to do business with this or presumably any other one guest in particular.

"I'll want a room not too far from the bathroom. Be stayin' maybe a couple nights. I'll let you know."

The clerk lifted his nose a bit so he could look down it. "All our guest accommodations have private sanitation facilities in the rooms. Tubs can be arranged in your room for an additional fifty cents."

"I'll be damned."

"Your judgment, sir. Not mine." The son of a bitch didn't even crack a smile when he said it. Raider wondered if maybe he should have gone to one of the cheaper places down the street. Still, he was here now. And a little extra privacy wasn't ever out of line. "How much for the room?"

"Three dollars."

"That the weekly or the monthly rate?"

The prig still didn't smile. He probably didn't have the foggiest idea that Raider was playing with him. "That would be the daily rate." He coughed delicately into a bunch-up little fist that looked just about right for crushing rose petals. When he got done with his coughing act he gave Raider a smug look that said he was expecting to see the back of Raider's coat any second now.

"Well, sonny"—the clerk was a good ten years older than Raider—"you trot me out a key an' have me some bath water sent up toot sweet." Raider'd heard Doc, his old partner, say shit like that. He wasn't just exactly sure what it meant, but he figured this prissy desk clerk could work it out. He gilded the lily a tad more by pulling out the wad of expense money Sigmond had given him and peeling off a crisp fifty. He flopped that onto the counter and told mister my-shit-don't-stink, "You let me know when that's used up, sonny."

"As you wish." Damned if fancy-pants didn't get the best of it, though. He never once blinked or changed expression or any way at all let on that he'd been pissing on the wrong fence post. The guy snapped his fingers, and a bellman came rushing out of the woodwork to take Raider's saddlebags and scabbarded Winchester.

"Room twenty-three, Willem. And an immediate tub."
The guy sucked air through his nose in a way that was
just short of a sniff. And a sniff would've gotten that
same nose rearranged over onto the side of his face.

"Right, mite." Old Willem, who looked to be twice
the desk clerk's age and near three times Raider's,
wasn't intimidated a lick by mister high-hat. He draped
the saddlebags comfortably over a shoulder and hefted
the Winchester like he'd maybe seen one of those things
before.

Raider winked at him, and the old fellow chuckled.

"After you, Willem."

"Oh, a'ter *you*, sor."

"Name's Raider."

"Name's Willem."

This time the snooty clerk did sniff. Raider was past
the notion to punch the dumb son of a bitch. He laughed
instead and walked with Willem to the stairs. The hell
with anybody that tight-puckered. Poor guy probably
had a terrible time trying to take a crap in the mornings.

Room twenty-three turned out to be on the third
floor, which was as far up as the hotel went. No doubt
the old boy downstairs thought he was giving Raider
some grief by giving him so many stairs to climb. Hell,
the day a couple stairs bothered him he might as well
quit hunting folks for a living. And being on the top
floor with no buildings as tall on either side would
make things unpleasant for anybody who might want to
lay an ambush for him while he was in his room.

"Cousin Jack?" Raider asked as he climbed the steps
slowly so he didn't outrun Willem.

"How'd ye guess?"

"Got you just a hint of accent left." Which was a
polite way of putting it. Actually the old boy's Welsh
accent was thick enough to spread with a knife.

"Aye. Been in the Colonies better'n forty years b'
now, though. S'prised ye could hear 't."

"Miner?"

"Aye. O' course. Driller. Then as I got th' age on me turned t' monkeyin' the powder." They reached the top landing, and Willem turned down the hall. "That lasted till I cut a fuse too short on' day. Tore up a fine young lad, I did. Boy lost an arm an' half 'is beardless face. Th' mine boss didn' give a shit. They all of 'em said 'twarn't my fault. Claimed it were bad fuse burnin' over-quick. Me, I knowed better. Hain't felt the sweet cool o' the stopes since nor smelt the powder an' rock dust. Been three year. Still miss it." He reached the door marked twenty-three, opened it and handed Raider the key. "I'll be gettin' your bath water first thing na, sor."

"Raider," the big man corrected.

"Aye. Raider."

"No need t' be in a hurry. Better yet, Willem, I could use a drink afore I get my bath. Whyn't you bring a bottle up an' we'll share a few afore you git t' thinkin' 'bout that water. Man needs some fortifyin' afore he hauls all that way."

"Ain't as bad as ye might think. Got a dumbwaiter, one o' them pulley things, t' get the buckets up here. Won't be s' bad." He winked. "Not 'at I'm turnin' ye down, mind."

Raider chuckled and gave the old man ten dollars of Roy Sigmond's money to buy the bottle with.

"Be back right short," Willem promised.

CHAPTER THIRTY-ONE

Raider felt considerably better when he walked out of the hotel late that afternoon. He'd had a bath, and his stomach was warm with a swallow or two from a clear glass pint bottle with no label on it. Whatever the liquor was, it was good. Old Willem hadn't had time to share it with him, though. Snoot-face'd had chores for the elderly bellman to do instead.

First stop was the telegraph office.

"I should have some messages. Name's Raider. I told the people at the other end to contact me by way of Evanston. You can get the retransmission from there."

"Raider, you say?"

"That's right."

"I'll put your request in to the Evanston operator soon as the line's open again." The Jasper operator wrote down the name and the request.

"Open again?"

"Line's down somewhere to the north, mister. I already have a man out looking for the break. Can't tell you just when he'll fix it, of course. Soon as he does, I'll be able to start transmitting again."

Raider grunted. There wasn't much you could do about something like that but wait. Line problems weren't so common any more, but they still happened. "Reckon I'll just have t' wait."

"Yes, sir. Like everybody else. If you like, I can send a boy to tell you when we have your messages in hand."

"I'd 'preciate that, friend." Raider gave the man the name of the fancy hotel and thanked him.

"Glad to be of service, sir."

Raider went back out onto the street and stood for a moment deciding where to go next. Jasper was big enough that strangers would be coming and going with some regularity. The arrival of a young couple in a mule-drawn wagon would cause no excitement here. Certainly Violet and Lester wouldn't have stopped at the expensive hotel where he was staying. If they had the funds to stop at a hotel at all. They could well have parked at the livery until they decided where to go. For that matter, they could have passed right on through without stopping at all if they had provisions enough to last them to wherever they were going.

Their destination might or might not be Jasper. Silver Canyon still? Likely not, he'd decided while he was riding today. If they'd been headed for Silver Canyon, surely they would have taken the fork through the gulch back on the other side of the mountains.

Where then? They could be going practically any-where in this corner of Utah, on into southwestern Wyoming, across into Brown's Hole in Colorado. The choices weren't exactly endless, but there were cer-tainly enough of them that Raider couldn't make any assumptions on the subject. He frowned.

What he was going to have to do, he supposed, was start tromping the sidewalks and hope he could find someone, a livery man or storekeeper or simply a pas-serby on the street who'd seen them and might be able to tell him whether they were staying or going on.

This kind of boring detail crap was exactly why Raider hated to get involved in penny ante little missing persons cases. A man got himself bogged down in nit-picking little stuff when he could be using his time for something really interesting instead. Still, this was the job he had to do. And standing on a street corner groaning about it wasn't going to get it done. He figured to start at one end of Jasper and work right on through to the next if that was what it took.

He walked up the street toward the livery at the edge of town where he'd left the dun horse.

CHAPTER THIRTY-TWO

The stores were closed and the streets nearly empty before Raider'd asked his questions along half the length of the main street in Jasper. The livery man hadn't been any more helpful than he was talkative, and the others Raider spoke to along the street were no better. Several of them refused to talk to him at all. The others professed to know nothing when they did give him a few minutes of their time. No one in Jasper seemed to have seen Violet Thorn or her husband or the wagon and mule or anything remotely resembling a young couple on the move. Raider hated to give it up. The Thorns might be right here in town this very minute. They could be a hundred yards from where he was standing, and he wouldn't know it. He seemed to have no choice, though, until the stores opened again tomorrow morning. Besides, by then the telegraph line to Evanston might be fixed and he could get some answers from Chicago.

He decided to settle for supper and a drink and a good night's sleep and ask through the rest of town come daylight. Supper would be no problem. From where he stood right now he could see one café and one somewhat more substantial restaurant, and the hotel had a restaurant section if he wanted to eat fancy.

Now that he thought about it, though, a drink was

going to be a little harder to find. There didn't seem to be a single damn saloon in the whole of Jasper. Be damned, Raider thought. It hadn't occurred to him before, but now that he was paying attention he realized he hadn't seen a bar nor heard a honky-tonk piano. Now what the hell kind of mining community was it, even a distant cousin to one like Jasper here, that didn't have a hell-raising district? That was strange. He walked out toward the smelter. There was smoke streaming from its oven stack, and lantern light through the windows showed that the smelter was operating a night shift. But even in that direction there wasn't a saloon operating. Raider grunted softly to himself and turned back toward the center of town. Not a red light to be seen around here either, and that was just as odd. With so many sheep wagons in evidence in Jasper there had to be sheepherders coming in now and again. And there should be cowboys wanting to get their ashes hauled before they left the bright lights behind. What the hell kind of strange place was this? Bunch of religious nuts?

Even fruitcakes have to eat, though. He stepped into the first greasy spoon he came to. The place was crowded with workmen from the smelter and some dark-haired fellows with gaudy bandannas who spoke a foreign tongue—not the Dutchie stuff he'd heard in the mountains but something else he guessed was Basque—and a smattering of ranch hands whose clothes and spurs and hat creases said north plains instead of Texas or the buckaroos from further west. Supper was served on the cheap, everybody sitting at one long table and the man with the longest, quickest reach making out the best when a fresh bowl or platter was set down. All the best spots at the table were already claimed, but there was always room for one more. And Raider wasn't shy about reaching. He made out all right.

Since he happened to be there anyway he asked his usual questions about Violet and Lester. Nobody's seen them. The men around the table ate fast and left quickly, so he had several different audiences to ask before he finally gave it up and paid for his meal.

The man who took his money dropped Raider's quarter into a grimy cigar box and glanced toward the table full of men to make sure no one was paying attention. Fat chance of that, of course. The boys gobbling down the groceries were only interested in one thing, and it took three red-faced, overworked women to keep up with the demand for full bowls.

"I heard you asking about a young couple new in town?" the man said in a near whisper.

"That's right."

"Saw a pair like that yesterday just before dark. They come down the road from Glory Hole and turned off south before they got to the livery. Didn't see where they went after that, of course. And it might not be the folks you're looking for. But there's some cabins down along the creek south of town. You might check down that way."

"Thanks."

The timing and the direction were certainly right. Raider grinned and thanked the café owner again.

"Hope it helps you out, mister."

If the tip paid off it wouldn't matter about the damn telegraph wire being down. He could find Violet and give her the news and escort her safely back to Silver Canyon. Allan Pinkerton could collect a fat fee from Roy Sigmond, and Raider could get back to some serious work.

He considered going back to the hotel for the Winchester. It was full dark by now, though, and a rifle is only an asset when you can make use of its greater range. That was hardly possible at night.

No point either in dragging the dun out of the livery at this hour. It would piss off the hostler and probably not accomplish anything.

The man at the café hadn't said how far it was to the cabins along the creek where Violet and Lester Thorn might be staying, but surely it couldn't be too far. The line of trees that indicated where the creek should be wasn't much more than a quarter mile past the lights of Jasper. Raider'd seen that much this afternoon when he was wandering around asking his questions. Raider figured it would be just as easy—and quieter—to walk the short distance. He cut across the street in the direction he thought he should go.

CHAPTER THIRTY-THREE

Son of a bitch!

He wasn't lost, of course. But he was damn sure confused for the time being.

He'd found the creek all right. Anybody with sense enough to walk downhill can generally find water in country where he knows there's supposed to be some. But finding those cabins was turning out to be more of a problem than Raider'd expected. There weren't any house lights to guide him. A body would think if there's a cabin and it's night and folks are living there, there just naturally should be some lamplight showing through a window or a door or a chink between the logs if nothing else. As far as Raider could see there wasn't a light of any sort this side of the last house in Jasper. Which he could see tantalizingly near up the slope as he edged his way back out of a clump of whippy, tangled willows. He'd blundered right into the damn things when he started down the last embankment above the creek, and now he was about hung up in the things in the dark. He would have wished for a lantern to light his way if it weren't for the fact that people'd been shooting at him lately. As it was he supposed he was more willing to put up with a willow switch across the face than a bullet between the shoulders. Question was, did he want to pick his way through the screen of

willows and search along the creek bank or climb back
up the bank and look for an easier way through.

Better to get on down by the creek and look along it,
he decided. If the willows, which he hadn't been able
to see from town earlier, were thick along this whole
stretch, they just might be thick enough that they were
blocking light from the cabins. That could be what was
throwing him off. Maybe if he could get past the willows and down along the creek he could see better.

He came to a complete stop and felt his way through
the thin, tangled branches six inches at a time until they
commenced to thin out. A thick canopy of cottonwood
branches was overhead now, blotting out the starlight
so that the creek bank was about as well lighted as the
inside of one of old Willem's mine stopes. Without the
head lamps.

Raider felt the willows give way to soft, leaf-littered
earth and then to fist-sized stones as he came closer to
the water. He could hear the creek running, the sound
of the water chuckling and burbling over the stones in
its bed. The air was cooler at the bottom of the cut
where the creek was, and the sound of the water traveled clear and far between the banks.

Raider stopped for a moment to listen, but there
wasn't any noise of pots or stove lids—or snoring, for
that matter—and he still couldn't spot any light down
here.

For all that he could see or hear he might as well be
three days ride back into the mountains instead of a
quarter mile from a town the size of Jasper.

The intense quiet, emphasized somehow by the merry
sounds of the rushing water, made him feel all the more
quiet and cautious himself. He eased back a few steps
to get away from the stones that lined the creek bed and
onto the softer soil under the cottonwoods.

Upstream from here? It was as good a guess as the
other. He'd reached the creek directly opposite the
town, and the man at the café said he saw the Thorns'

wagon turn off west of town instead of coming on through. Raider had a fifty-fifty chance of being right whichever way he decided to go.

He turned to his right, toward the west, and felt his way slowly and quietly along the fringe of the thick willows.

He hadn't gone a hundred yards before he stopped again and shrank down beside the willows with a hand on the butt of the big Remington.

"What the hell's keeping him?" The voice was a low, hoarse whisper that carried well between the creek banks.

"Shut up, man. Just be quiet and watch that path."

"Wish that damn moon would come up."

"Did I tell you to shut up?"

"But—"

"Quiet." The second voice was sharp and insistent this time. The first one shut up.

My oh my, now. Wasn't this interesting?

There was a sound of boot heels grating on gravel and a soft, grunting sigh. Raider guessed somebody'd got tired of standing and sat down for a spell instead. Somebody with a rifle or a shotgun, maybe? It did seem likely.

He'd been wondering what became of those boys from Creel City. He was beginning to think maybe he'd found them again, down here along the creek, waiting beside a path that Raider hadn't known about. Expecting him—or somebody—to come along from the direction of Jasper.

Yes indeed he did think this was mighty interesting. The next question was what to do about it.

CHAPTER THIRTY-FOUR

There were two quick and easy solutions that came immediately to mind. One was to slither up there behind those boys and cut them down before they realized they weren't alone out here in the night. The other was to just back away and go somewhere else. Let them sit here getting mosquito bites the whole night through if that's what they wanted. There were problems with both those possibilities, though.

The biggest thing wrong with the first idea, to blow them away and be done with it, was that Raider didn't know for sure that it was him those men were laying for. Or, for that matter, he didn't know for sure that it was any human person they were waiting for out here in the bushes. He thought back over the few whispered words he'd heard and had to admit that all he really heard was two fellas hiding by a path. They could be innocent, respectable townspeople from Jasper trying to get a shot at a chicken-stealing coyote that'd been eating their breakfast egg supply too many nights. Raider didn't believe that. Not for a minute. But it could be. He didn't want to become the kind of dipshit son of a bitch that would backshoot civilians just because he thought he was in some personal danger. So no, walking up on them and putting them out of their misery was pretty much out of the running when it came to bright ideas here.

On the other hand, knowing they were there and just moseying quietly off into the night didn't particularly appeal to him either. If he did that he wouldn't ever know for sure who they were or what they wanted. If they were innocent locals or a pair of shooters from Creel City. If it was him they wanted or a hungry coyote, or for that matter if they were hired guns looking for somebody else entirely. Not very damned likely, of course. All the less so the more he thought about it.

Just how many folks would there likely be in Jasper tonight who'd been set up for an ambush down by the creek? Because at this point Raider was sure beginning to think he'd been set up by that man back at the café. There damn sure weren't any signs of cabins down here where that man had said the Thorns were supposed to be stopping at a cabin.

Apparently there was a path, though Raider hadn't seen it on his way down. Lucky for him he'd come straight on from town instead of walking out the road above the livery and finding the path that café owner had so carefully directed him to. The one with the gunmen waiting beside it.

This whole smelly thing pointed to one more attempt to get to him before he could reach Violet and Lester Thorn, wherever the hell they were. This was getting more confusing all the time.

Raider thought over his two good possibilities and rejected both of them. He couldn't just shoot down two people who by a remote stretch of the imagination could be innocent bystanders. He just damn well wasn't going to do that. But he wasn't going to walk away from them either and wait for them to lay a better ambush the next time. If these were the boys who'd been trying for him all the way from Salt Lake there would sure as hell be a next time. Given a choice,

Raider would prefer to end it here than go along waiting for them to eventually get lucky.

He fingered the grip of the Remington but left the big gun in its holster and took his hand away. These boys weren't all that good at playing games at night in the woods or Raider wouldn't know they were there right now. For what he had in mind something a little quieter than a cartridge seemed in order.

He smiled grimly to himself and took a cautious step forward. Then another.

CHAPTER THIRTY-FIVE

He knew roughly where they were. He needed to know precisely where each man was. Time, though, was on Raider's side. The two shooters thought they were alone here. Only Raider knew better. As long as he stayed quiet he could take advantage of any noise they made. And given enough time, any but a solid professional was going to fuck up.

Raider left the soft, leafy soil under the cottonwoods and moved slowly into the willow thicket. Absolute silence was what he had to have here, even if it took him two hours to move ten feet into the willows. A two hour investment was small pay when a man's neck was on the line.

The willows weren't quite as thick here as those he'd come through downstream. By oozing forward a fraction of an inch at a time he was able to slide through the slender branches without noise. The biggest danger in here was the sound of leaves scraping over his clothes whenever he moved far enough for a snagged branch to slide free and whip back to its natural placement. Raider moved only inches at a time. His hands were busy locating and pulling aside the branches as he came to them, carefully finding each one, disengaging it from his pants legs and moving it behind him so he could go forward just a little bit more. It was slow and tedious, but impatience here could lead to a gunshot out of the night. Raider figured he could put up with tedium better than with bullets.

It took him a half hour or more to get inside the willow thicket to a point he thought was behind the man on this side of the path. By then it was hard to recall just exactly where the whispered voices had come from.

He heard a man cough.

"Shhh."

Raider smiled. Thank you very much, gentlemen.

One was thirty or so feet in front of him. That would be on the far side of the narrow path they were watching. The answering warning came from twelve or fifteen feet straight ahead. That would be the one on the near side. The smarter and more wary one at that. Perfect.

Raider ghosted through the willows like a night mist, slow and silent. There wasn't a hint of light to guide him, but he had the men's positions fixed now. Ten feet to go. Eight.

Raider could feel his belly tighten and turn cold. He rubbed a palm across the leg of his trousers to dry it, then removed another willow branch and eased it around behind him. Six inches gained. He was smiling again.

What he had in mind was to get to within a foot or two of the nearer man and take him down hard and fast. But not permanent. Raider wanted to have a talk with these boys.

He could deal with the other one however it played once he had his hands on the first one. First thing was to get the nearer man alive and immobile.

Six feet. Four.

He couldn't see shit in front of him, but he could sense the presence of the shooter. Could smell the man's dried sweat on his clothes. The man was no rough country professional. He'd gotten a haircut today. Raider could smell a faint, lingering scent of the weak lotion barbers use when they shave the back of a customer's neck below the hair line. A first class shooter would have thought about that. Would have waited until tomorrow to visit the barber.

Raider edged a few inches closer over the sloping, uneven ground of the creek bank. He found and removed three more willow branches. He was careful of his breathing now. The temptation was always to breathe through your mouth when you were trying to be really quiet. A man can hear his own breathing through his nose. But that's because his nose and ears both connect in his throat. Unless a guy is a real snorter he can't be heard breathing through his nose. But mouth breathing can be heard by someone else even when a guy isn't aware of it himself. A guy can actually be panting and not know it when he's keyed up and nervous.

Raider was so close behind the guy now that it was amazing the shooter couldn't sense his presence behind the man's back.

The man was breathing normally. Raider could hear it. The guy wasn't nervous or worried. Just bored. That was about to change.

Raider knew where the man was. Could almost but not quite see him in the intense shadows of the thicket. He knew where the guy's body was, but he had to determine precisely where the man's head was. This one had to go down quickly, with no fuss at all, if there was any hope of getting both of them.

Raider hunkered down into a crouch, trying to find some paler shadows behind the man's bulk to silhouette him against. To find that head and neck and set himself just right. Damn, it was dark. A little moonlight would be mighty welcome right about now.

The stalk had taken more than an hour already. Why in hell wasn't this guy getting bored and moving around some? He ought to be by now. Patient son of a bitch.

Maybe if Raider shifted to the side a little. A few inches. A foot. Just so he could—

A stone buried in the loose topsoil shifted under his

boot. Raider's ankle turned and he lurched sideways, off balance for a split second.

He caught himself with a loud crackle of dead leaves underfoot.

"Wha—?"

The man Raider was stalking must've thought the hounds of Hell were coming at him out of the night. He jumped half out of his skin, rising to full height and spinning around. Raider could see him when he moved. He had something long and dark in his hands.

"Harvey?" The guy on the other side of the path sounded nervous.

Raider lunged forward, fist swinging, bringing a hard one out of the darkness straight for the shooter's balls. Immobilize this bastard quick and concentrate on the other one. His fist sank deep into the man's crotch, Raider grunting with the effort he put behind it and the shooter grunting with the shock of unexpected agony.

"Harvey?"

The man Raider'd hit staggered backward, clutching himself, his finger closing involuntarily on the triggers of the gun he was carrying, and two large barrels of deadly shot bellowed and spat lead into the trees. The muzzle flash illuminated the willows and the overhanging cottonwoods for fifteen or twenty feet around.

Raider blinked, his night vision destroyed by the sudden burst of bright light.

Shit!

On the other side of the path the second man panicked. Another shotgun roared in the night. Harvey screamed and fell writhing into the path he'd been watching.

"Harvey? Oh, Jesus an' Joseph. Harvey?"

Raider dropped belly down to the ground a split second before the man cut loose his second barrel.

Lead pellets whipped and tore through the willows over his head.

He had the big Remington in hand, but he had no target, dammit.

He still couldn't see a damn thing after the flashes of light.

Harvey was moaning and screaming, thrashing on his back in the middle of the path.

"Harvey?"

The questioning sound was followed moments later by the sound of something large and heavy moving fast through the willows. Up the bank to open, level ground. Then footsteps fast receding.

Raider knelt low to the ground for a moment, finger-tips pressed against his eyes. He blinked and shook his head, trying to will his night vision to return.

Harvey continued to groan. The sounds of his breathing were loud and labored.

Raider came to his feet and moved forward again. But this time there was no need at all for silence. He knelt and frisked Harvey quickly for weapons. The shotgun the man was still holding was empty. Raider found and tossed into the willows a small, nickel clad rimfire revolver.

His hands came away wet and sticky from where he'd touched Harvey's torso while searching him.

The labored, bubbling sounds issuing from Harvey's throat when he breathed said the man wasn't going to be breathing very much longer. The pellets from the other guy's shotgun had torn into Harvey's lungs and who knew how much more. Raider didn't have a helluva lot of time to ask questions of this one. He took a chance that the other gunman was still more interested in running than in turning back to fight a wraith in the night. He pulled out a lucifer and snapped the sulfur tip with a thumbnail, lighting the path with its flare. Raider held it down close to Harvey's twisting, agonized features as he gulped for air like a beached trout.

"Shit," Raider said aloud in the night.

CHAPTER THIRTY-SIX

Raider had seen this man before somewhere. Knew him or at least had talked with him.

Harvey. It took him a moment to remember where and when. The dying man was the City Hall clerk Raider'd talked to back in Salt Lake when he was first looking for Violet Thorn there. Raider couldn't remember his last name. Harvey'd been dressed differently then. Very proper. Very businesslike. And he'd been very pleasant and helpful. Courteous and informative. Now he was dressed for the trail. And packing deadly weapons. Now he was part of the effort to kill Raider and must have been part of it all the way here from Salt Lake. Before Creel City and since. But he wasn't alone, damn it. The battle below the gulch proved that.

Raider remembered now that this man had tried to point him right then toward the carpenter Lester Thorn when Raider asked his first questions about Violet Sigmond.

It had taken Raider a while longer to become interested in Lester, though. He hadn't acted immediately on this man's suggestion. And by the time he did the Thorns were gone from Salt Lake and there was an ambush waiting for Raider there at the old building he was so carefully directed to. Hell, this Harvey must've

151

been trying to set him up right from Raider's first question at the city hall building.

But what the fuck for?

Who knew beforehand that there would be someone interested in the whereabouts of Violet Sigmond Thorn and why would they be wanting to stop that someone from finding her? This Harvey must have been prepared in advance about what to do when someone came to him. If he was ready, then surely others must have been briefed and ready too. In any number of places where a Pinkerton operative might ask questions.

But why would a city employee in Salt Lake give a shit about it? And how many others were prepared to give information and set ambushes? Who were they? And why? That many people couldn't have so great a personal hatred against one young woman as to justify all of this.

The match burned down to Raider's fingernails and he lighted another. He picked up a dead willow switch and lit off the match to serve as a makeshift torch.

"Harvey? Can you hear me, Harvey?"

Waters. That was the guy's name. Harvey Waters. It came back to him when he tried to talk to the dying man.

"Mr. Waters?"

Harvey Waters was much more interested in his pain than he was in Raider's voice. His head rolled and jerked back and forth as the pain consumed him.

The front of his shirt was bloody although there were only a few holes in the cloth that Raider could see. Those, though, were exit holes. The second man's charge of heavy shot must have taken Waters full in the back, riddling his lungs before a few of the pellets burst all the way through. The rest of them would be lodged somewhere inside his body.

"Waters. Damn it, man, you have to tell me. Why? You have to tell me."

Waters's eyes rolled toward him. The man looked at Raider for the first time. Seemed to recognize him.

"Tell me, man. What do you have against Violet? Why are you tryin' t' stop me from helpin' her?"

Harvey Waters' eyes opened wider. In disbelief? Questioning? Certainly not with hate. Raider was sure about that.

Waters's lips parted. He tried to speak. Pale, frothy blood filled his mouth. He tried to swallow it back. He was drowning in his own blood. He tried to say something. Waters's hand clamped around Raider's wrist, and he tried to pull himself up. To make himself heard.

All Raider heard was a hissing groan.

"Tell me, man."

Waters collapsed.

His hand fell limply away from Raider's wrist, and his eyes went blank and sightless.

Raider shook out the small flame at the tip of the dry willow twig, and the path was plunged again into darkness.

Somewhere down the creek an owl chuckled in the night.

CHAPTER THIRTY-SEVEN

Raider slept well that night. But not before he bolted the hotel room door and lugged the bed from its usual position against an inside wall to one near the window, where no one could shoot through the thin wallboards and nail him without ever showing themselves. That done, though, he slept deeply and without remorse.

When he woke, he figured he needed some breakfast. And he couldn't think of a more interesting place to get it than at that café where the owner had been so *helpful* the night before.

The place had been locked up tight when he got back to town last night, leaving Harvey Waters dead where he fell. Waters's pal could come back and claim the body if he wanted. Raider didn't want to get into that and most certainly didn't want to get into any long discussions with the local law about who'd shot whom over what during the night. If the people who were trying to ambush Raider had connections in Salt Lake City's local government they sure had the clout it would take to run a ringer into a place like Jasper.

Raider shit and shaved—it was something of a treat to be able to do both right there in the privacy of his own hotel room—and bypassed the hotel restaurant on his way out.

The morning was bright and fine.

And the damn café several blocks down was closed up tight.

There was no note posted on the door to indicate when the place would reopen or why it was closed—although Raider had a few guesses he might've passed along if anybody'd been interested—and while Raider was there, several workmen tried to go in and grumbled and cussed when they found the door padlocked.

The helpful SOB at the counter had skipped.

Probably the second shotgunner beat his feet for the café last night when the ambush failed. By now both of them would be holed up and not show again until the Pinkerton man left Jasper.

Raider was disappointed but not exactly surprised. He got a quick breakfast instead at the next restaurant he saw. No one stepped forward to help him there, but nobody shot at him either. Then he went down the street to the telegraph office. He was waiting outside when the telegrapher opened his doors.

"Mr. Raider. Good morning." The man smiled and welcomed him in.

"Mornin'."

"I haven't any news for you yet, Mr. Raider. Sorry."

Raider grunted.

"I haven't forgotten you, though. First thing when that line opens, I'll send a boy to the hotel for you."

"Thanks."

Raider glanced behind the telegrapher to the desk where the big brass and steel key was mounted. A few papers lay beside the clicker, and the remains of the operator's breakfast were spread out nearby. The key perched silent and useless in the center of it all.

"I don't s'pose you'd know—"

The telegrapher shrugged and smiled again. "Sorry. I wish I could tell you."

"Yeah. Thanks. I'll, uh, check back with you later."

"You do that, Mr. Raider."

Raider let himself out and walked up the street to the livery, making a stop first at the hotel.

He saddled the dun, strapped the Winchester scabbard under his leg and set off away from Jasper at a slow, easy lope toward the northeast.

Raider pulled the dun to a stop and looked behind him. Far enough, he judged. Jasper was well out of sight several hills back. And the rolling country here was open and barren of obvious cover. It wasn't the sort of spot an amateur would choose for a stalk or an ambush.

He dismounted and led the dun horse to the nearest telegraph pole and tied it there.

The thin line of poles and wire ran behind him less than two miles to Jasper and ahead for many more miles to Evanston, Wyoming, and points beyond.

The damn poles were thin all right, though. Scrawny things barely bigger than saplings. That was a nuisance. Raider hated climbing spindly, undersized little poles like this. The things had no climbing pins screwed into them, and he didn't have any boot spikes, so he was undoubtedly in for some splinters.

He took his hat off, slipped a coil of insulated wire into a pocket and pulled his gloves on.

At least the damn pole wasn't particularly tall. Fifteen feet or so. All he had to do was shin up to the telegraph line and tap into it with his own wire. Thank goodness the real work involved, raising the Evanston operator and getting his messages transmitted to him, could be done comfortably from ground level. He had wire enough to run a drop to his portable key while he sat and took his time with the chore.

Raider smiled, the expression tight and grim. Damn telegrapher back in Jasper must think he was some kind of idiot. The stack of overnight outgoing that Raider'd seen yesterday was gone from the operator's desk now. And there were fresh message forms in the incoming basket. Wire down my ass, Raider thought. Whoever it was that didn't want him finding Violet Thorn was still trying to play games.

He looked the pole over, trying to decide which side was the least gouged and splintered, then started carefully up.

CHAPTER THIRTY-EIGHT

Raider folded the sheaf of paper he'd covered with hurried scrawling and tucked it into a pocket. The message from Chicago was in code, and he didn't want to take the time out here to sit down and work it out.

Unless the operator in Jasper was keeping his key turned off to maintain the illusion that there was no telegraph service to the town—unlikely when the Pinkerton man had ridden away hours earlier—he and anyone else he wanted to tell knew long since that Raider was transmitting on their wire. There was no way to hide the fact. The impulses ran in both directions on that wire, and in order to raise the Evanston operator Raider had to let the Jasper operator listen in too. That was why he'd asked Evanston only for the coded message from Chicago and never mind anything from Roy Sigmond.

Receiving the full text had taken some time. Plenty long enough for an ambush party to be riding the line by now. The Chicago message was an unusually long one, and a coded message is always harder to take down accurately than a plain language one because you can't anticipate what the next letters will be. Plain language you could often read with only a few letters sent. In code you never knew what symbol might come next.

Raider'd had to break the Evanston operator's rhythm several times to ask him to slow down or to repeat sections. All in all, Raider figured he'd been on the line three quarters of an hour or more before he finally had the message in his pocket and could ride away.

He tugged on the tap wire to bring it down—damn sure better than climbing that splintery pole again, and the hell with that guy in Jasper if Raider accidentally grounded the line for him—and coiled it again. He stowed the wire and key in his saddlebags and untied the dun.

The horse was restive and eager for work after good feed and so much rest. It bogged its head and tried to shake him when he mounted. No serious intent about that. The animal was literally feeling its oats and wanting to get playful.

Raider let it have its head and moved southeast at an easy gallop that would burn off some surplus energy without tiring the horse. He held the dun to that for a mile and then dropped it back to a lope, moving steadily farther from the line of telegraph poles.

If the telegrapher and his friends were out looking for Raider they would be following the poles to find him. Raider didn't figure to be there, and he didn't intend to make their job any easier for them by riding the line back to them.

This was country he hadn't covered before. The Uinta Mountains rose bulky and seemingly barren to the west and north, and a near dry basin spread off to the east. As far as Raider knew that stretch extended all the way into Brown's Hole in Colorado.

Angling off from south by southwest toward east by northeast he could see a snaky, wandering line of green.

That, he figured, would be a downstream extension of the creek where Waters and friend had spent the evening last night.

He could ride to that and turn upstream to make his way back to Jasper under the cover of the creek bank's foliage.

CHAPTER THIRTY-NINE

Well now. How the hell about that?

Raider stepped off the dun and led it into a dense tangle of chokecherries and tied it there. The horse didn't like the feel of the branches scraping its flanks, but Raider had more interesting things to think about than what the rented horse liked or didn't like.

He secured the dun out of sight and slid the Winchester out of the scabbard.

Upstream a hundred yards or so he'd spotted a roof. And then once he got to paying close attention, through the thick underbrush he could see, in another spot altogether, a glimpse of log wall. There seemed to be several cabins built along the creek between him and Jasper, which he figured to be better than a mile away after the circuitous route he'd taken to get here.

What he found so really interesting about that little discovery was the tale he'd been fed by that man at the café last night trying to draw him under a shotgun muzzle. The easiest kind of lie to think up, and the easiest kind to keep track of afterward, is a lie that's based on a grain of truth, with just a bit of imagination to carry the liar on from there. Now it just could be that the old boy at the café last night had made up an easy lie, and these isolated cabins were the worm of truth that was hidden inside the liar's bad apple. The

man'd said Violet and Lester turned off the road south
of Jasper and likely were headed toward some imagi-
nary old cabins along the creek. Damned well interesting, Raider thought, that now he was finding some
cabins along the creek northeast of town.

Could there be a connection? He was going to find
out.

On foot and under cover, Raider slipped through the
brush toward the cabins. When he got close enough to
see them better, it was easy to tell they weren't inhabited. Not on a regular basis, anyway. There were four
of them standing, and he could see several foundations
and abandoned chimney stubs that showed there had
been more at some time in the past—ten, maybe twelve
all told—but now there were only four left upright and
more or less intact.

A clutch of old buildings like this wasn't uncommon
around towns. The earliest settlers would come into a
brand new piece of country and locate directly on water
and in a place where they could secure wood without
having to walk for it too far. Like, for instance, right
smack on the banks of a clear-running creek.

Then later on the population would grow, and all that
would change. Roads'd be cut so it was easier to haul
wood by mule and wagon and a man didn't have to
have his own woodlot outside his door. There'd be
people upstream shitting in the creek, so a man wanted
a well instead of a dipper for his water. Stores and
proper houses would be built where it was easiest to
build roads. And so a place like Jasper would grow up
close to where there used to be just a handful of crude
cabins, and the old community would be abandoned in
favor of the modern town. This right here looked like
just such a deal.

Raider moved higher on the slope of the creek bank
and shifted closer.

Three of the remaining four cabins still had roofs or
parts of roofs. The fourth was just four walls, he could

see from this new angle. Two of them had shutters still
at their windows.

Seemed entirely possible that Violet and Lester might
be inside one of these places, even though Raider couldn't
see any sign of a mule and wagon, and there wasn't any
smoke in the air that he could see or smell. They could
be here if that café man was telling his lie with a kernel
of truth buried in the middle of it. Though it still didn't
make a hell of a lot of sense.

If the men from Salt Lake and Creel City and now
Jasper were trying to kill Raider, why the hell should
Violet and Lester be known to them and safe from
them? Raider was trying to assist the Thorns, even
though they didn't know it. If those quick-to-shoot
SOBs knew enough about Raider to know he was looking for the Thorns, how was it they wouldn't know he
was trying to help them? Best way to work that out,
Raider decided, was to find Violet and Lester and ask
them.

He edged forward a little closer to the cabins. There
were only two of them that would likely be inhabited—if,
indeed, anyone was here at all—and to reach either of
them he would have to expose himself to view from the
other. If he picked the wrong cabin to sneak up on, he
could get a real rude welcome from a window or wall
chink of the other place. Those Salt Lake boys were
altogether too fond of shotguns for Raider's taste.

He settled down under a wild plum and put on his
patient hunter's face, prepared for as long a wait as it
took to tell him which and whether one of those two
cabins was occupied.

CHAPTER FORTY

The door of the cabin on the right opened, and a man came out.

Raider smiled and shifted his grip on the stock of the Winchester.

The café owner knew about these cabins, all right. Because there the son of a bitch stood. The man paused in a patch of shade-dappled sunshine and admired the flirting of a squirrel's tail on a branch overhead, then walked behind a tumbledown chimney with no walls around it and took a piss. He was careful to position himself so he couldn't be seen from the cabin, and Raider smiled again. That indicated that there was a woman inside the cabin. Otherwise the café owner would likely just whiz it out the door and never mind getting out of sight. It remained to be seen if that woman was Violet Thorn. But the probability sure looked high.

The café owner hadn't changed clothes since the last time Raider saw him. He must have rushed here to hide when he found out his little trick didn't work. Hadn't armed himself either. He was in suspenders and shirtsleeves, and there was no sign of a gun anywhere on him.

The guy finished his business, buttoned up, and went back inside, leaving the cabin door standing open.

Raider checked the terrain along the creek. The large trees had been thinned out when the community of cabins was a going concern, and the clearing had grown back to underbrush and healthy saplings. There was cover enough for a man to get around to the back of that cabin without being seen if he took his time about it and paid attention to what he was doing.

Raider hefted the Winchester and moved out low to the ground. He made a wide sweep around behind the cabin and came up close to it.

By the time he was where he wanted to be there was a curl of pale smoke rising from the cracked, sagging chimney. Lunchtime. Someone—Violet?— was preparing a meal. For how many, though? Raider wished he knew.

He hunkered close to the back wall of the cabin, directly underneath a window frame that had never seen a pane of glass although there were still some tattered remnants of oiled paper stuck in the cracks around it.

"—bacon or sausage?" It was a woman's voice. Raider only caught the tail end of the question.

"Bacon please, ma'am." That one was a voice that sounded familiar. Raider thought it was the man who'd been calling out Harvey's name in the dark last night. The one who'd shot Harvey Waters down by mistake.

"For me too, honey." That was a voice Raider was sure he'd never heard before. Definitely not the café owner nor the ambusher. Lester Thorn? That was only a guess, so he put that one aside for the moment.

"What about you, Avery?" the women asked.

"Bacon will be fine, thank you." Raider was positive that was the café owner.

Polite bunch, weren't they. Not like old or close friends. They knew each other, obviously. And they were all hiding out here together. From him. But they didn't know each other well enough to be loose and easy together.

"Shouldn't I cook enough for—" The woman let the

question die, and afterward there was a silence that Raider suspected was awkward and uncomfortable for the people inside the hideout.

After a moment someone coughed.

"I'm sorry," the woman's voice said. "I didn't mean—"

"Look," that was Avery, the café man, "let's face the truth here. Harvey won't be joining us. The angels got him."

The angels got him? Funny way of putting it, Raider thought. Especially since Avery's tone of voice had more than a touch of bitterness in it when he added that last sentence.

The angels got him. But like he was accusing, not like he was saying something comforting and religious.

"I'm sorry," the woman repeated.

Raider could hear a pot or skillet scraping on iron, and a whiff of bacon just beginning to heat reached him through the open window. It'd been a long while since breakfast by now, and the good smell got his mouth to watering.

How the hell was he going to get in there and talk to Violet and Lester—if, indeed, that was who was inside there, just a few feet beyond the logs Raider was leaning against—without Avery or the other unknown shotgunner trying to cut him down?

He sure as hell didn't want to go in shooting.

Shit, he didn't even know which man in there would be Lester Thorn and which would be the man who wanted to kill him. Avery he would recognize from the café but not either of the other men.

And he hadn't come this far just to fuck up and shoot Violet's husband in front of her eyes.

The object here was to help her, not to destroy her life.

If he waited until they were all gathered around the table, he decided, he could come in quiet and easy, with the Winchester left outside and no noise or intimidation.

Maybe, just maybe, he could get some talking in before everyone began shooting.

Raider tilted his Stetson back and sat down beside the cabin wall. He would wait out here however long it took. About all he could do beyond that was cross his fingers and hope.

CHAPTER FORTY-ONE

Something hit the wood beside Raider's ear with a sound like an ax blade thumping into a dry log.

Except this wasn't any ax, and a moment later there was the sharp crack of a rifle shot.

Raider threw himself sideways and rolled behind the side of the cabin.

Beside the creek and sixty or seventy yards upstream he could see a man on horseback working the lever on a saddle carbine for another shot.

Behind the rider were more horses and men. Three, four, perhaps more of them.

Raider palmed his Remington and threw a shot in the general direction of the riders.

Inside the cabin he could hear shouts and pounding feet.

Raider tried to look around the back of the cabin toward the creek and was greeted by a fusillade of bullets and flying splinters.

"Damn!"

He pulled back, moving toward the front of the cabin. By the time he got to that end of the building, the place was empty. He could see the backs of the people, a slim young woman among them, disappearing into the brush upstream where the horsemen could cover their retreat.

The men had come along the creek bed and spotted Raider lurking beside the cabin before he could get inside and talk to Violet and Lester.

Damn and double damn, he thought.

The riders were probably the party sent out to search the telegraph line for him. When they didn't find him they came back this way, either to warn the people in the cabin or to inform them. They hadn't followed Raider here or they would have come from the downstream side of the cabin and Raider probably would have spotted them before they were aware he was here. He'd been looking in that direction but mostly listening to what was going on inside the cabin while he waited for the group to settle at the table.

Now the whole thing was blown. Violet and Lester would be on the move again. And he hadn't any idea which direction they might run in next.

Why the hell were they running from him anyway?

He eased along the front cabin wall and peered around the corner. There was only one rider visible there now. He sat with his carbine leveled, watching the back end of the cabin where Raider was last seen.

The other horsemen had pulled back. Raider could hear them moving through the thick growth beyond the clearing. Could hear voices. Shouts. Greetings. Apparently the horsemen were picking up the woman and three men from the cabin and hurrying them to safety.

The one who was on guard was intent on the back of the cabin while Raider was at the front on the other side of the building. The guard had no idea he was being observed. Raider braced his wrist against the notched log ends at the corner of the cabin and took a careful bead. At this distance from a steady rest the man with the carbine was as good as dead. A three or four inch compensation for bullet drop, a gentle squeeze and the guy would have one through the chest. Raider could shoot his teeth out at this range, and the man wouldn't have time to know it happened. Raider took aim. Then he lifted his finger from the trigger.

There was something—dammit, he wanted to know more before he started cutting these people down. They all obviously thought they were protecting Violet and Lester. They all, Violet and Lester included, obviously believed that Raider presented a threat to the young couple. Those people were on the run. From Raider. Their actions said they thought they were defending themselves from him.

And something just damn sure didn't fit about all this. Something Raider'd learned a hell of a long time ago was that when your conclusions don't fit the facts, some damn thing has to be out of whack.

Either your conclusions are all balled up, or your facts are.

At this point he was becoming pretty well convinced that Violet Thorn was running like hell to get away from him. And that her husband and all their friends in strange places were genuinely convinced that they were helping Violet by trying to stop Raider. That was a conclusion. So where did that lead the facts Raider thought he knew? Something, someplace along the line, was commencing to smell bad. He holstered the Remington and tapped the pocket that was bulky with the coded message from Chicago. Maybe he could learn something from that.

He stood at the corner of the cabin and watched patiently while somewhere upstream there was a shout, and immediately the rider with the carbine turned and spurred his horse away in the direction Violet and Lester Thorn had just fled. The withdrawal only served to reinforce Raider's conviction that what these people wanted wasn't so much his death as it was Violet's safety. They had enough guns with them this time that they could have laid siege to him if they'd wanted. Instead their primary concern was to get Violet out of danger and then withdraw without forcing a fight of it.

Raider gave them ample time to get well clear of the neighborhood, then went inside and helped himself to a sandwich of hot bacon and fresh bread that he munched on his way back downstream to where he'd hidden the dun. He wanted to get back to the privacy—and for that matter the safety—of his hotel room so he could decode the wire from Chicago and maybe find some answers to all these inconsistencies. And at this point he would prefer it if he could manage that without having to shoot Lester Thorn or any of his pals.

CHAPTER FORTY-TWO

Raider met the elderly bellman Willem in the third floor hallway.

"Raider." The old miner nodded.

"Hello, Willem."

"I was, um, wondering if ye'd like to share that drink ay couldn't have yesterd'y."

"Sure, Willem."

The old fellow grinned. Raider unlocked the door and let the bellman in. The bottle Willem had produced yesterday—no mean feat considering that there didn't seem to be any place in town that sold the stuff—was on the dresser.

There was only one chair in the room. Willem stood until Raider motioned him into it and sat on the side of the bed. "To your good health, Willem." He took a pull.

"An' t' yours, Raider." The old man accepted the bottle and drank from it. "For as long as it lasts, 'at is."

Raider lifted an eyebrow.

"Old men hear things, ye see," Willem said.

"That so?"

"Aye. Time t' time." He drank again.

"And, uh, what is it old men hear time t' time?" Raider was beginning to suspect that the chance meeting in the hallway hadn't been so chancy after all. Another setup by Violet's protectors? It was certainly possible. If Willem wanted to send him to some out of the way place now—

Willem passed the bottle back. It was good stuff. Raider helped himself to a dose of seconds.

"You got t' understand that there's an element o' us hereabouts as ain't saints," Willem said.

"Shit, Willem, I ain't no saint m'self." He looked at the bottle in his hand and winked. Then grinned. "Aside from the demon rum here, I been known t' fancy the company of fast horses an' faster women too."

Willem smiled. Then quickly sobered. "You mistake me, Raider."

"How's that?"

"Saints, mon. Moor-mons. Most folks hereabout is Moor-mon, y'see."

Moor-mon. It took him a moment. Mormon. But hell yes, most of Utah and the country on all sides of it was Mormon. So what? He did remember, though, that the Mormons referred to themselves as saints. And come to think of it, they were opposed to liquor too. Not that any of that seemed important when it came to the case of Violet Thorn and her groundless fears.

"What's your point, Willem?" Raider liked the old man. But he had work to do, and sitting here enjoying a midafternoon drink wasn't getting that wire decoded.

"You ain't so popular a man wi' some o' them Moor-mons, Raider. Wi' the saints. An' yet I hear ye're almighty favored by th' angels."

Raider blinked and sat up straighter. "Angels?"

"Aye. T'other bunch o' Moor-mons."

Angels! That voice in the cabin had said something about Harvey Waters being taken by the angels. Could he have meant that some way other than the one Raider thought?

"Who the fuck are these angels, Willem?"

"Don' know these Moor-mons, eh, lad?"

"No. But I'd damn sure like you t' tell me."

"Aye, I c'n do 'at. I come here t' warn ye, see. Expect I c'n educate ye too."

"B'lieve me, Willem, I'd 'preciate that." He handed the bottle back to the old man. There wasn't much left in it. Willem was damn well welcome to all there was, and to whatever else Raider could find to please him, if he could help clarify the inconsistencies about Violet Thorn and her brother Roy Sigmond.

"Use' t' be jus' the one bunch, see. Joseph Smith. Brigham Young. Them boys. Set theyselves up as saints, see, an' invited ever'body else t' tag onto their coattails."

"Sure. I've heard o' them o' course."

"Then a while back, see, when it turned out 'ey couldn't make this here patch o' desert an' mountain inta a separate country all it's own, they d'cided 'ey wanted t' become a state instead. Ye heard 'bout that, I s'pose?"

"Sorta." There were a number of things that Raider really didn't give a crap about. Politics was high on that list. Mostly politics seemed to be an exercise in crime at a level higher than he could fight, so he ignored it.

"Right. So 'ey wanted t' become a state out here. But back in th' States, the Supreme Court, it says 'ey can't do that 'cause of havin' too many wives fer each man."

That part Raider had certainly heard about. Some of those old time Mormons had wives by the dozens. Literally. Which didn't show much in the way of judgment that Raider could see. He couldn't understand why a man would want to put up with one full time wife, much less a bunch of them all lumped together. The reasoning sure couldn't have to do with the variety of available pussy. A man could have all of that that he wanted without marrying them in droves, for crying out loud.

"So back in th' States," Willem went on, helping himself to another nip, "they say these Moor-mons gotta cut back t' one wife apiece in their laws if they wanta become another state, see.''

Raider nodded. He remembered about that, though he'd never paid any particular attention to the details.

''So out here, see, there's some as say it's their God-given religious right t' have as many wives as they please. Them is the old line Moor-mons, see. An' then there's this other bunch as wants t' become a state an' change their ways. So what happens? Religious revelation, see, it comes in real convenient sometimes.'' The old man cackled and drained the last of the liquor.

''What happens is, lo an' behold, there's this new an' improved religious revelation from on high, see. An' all o' a sudden these saints—ye got t' understand they all figger they can chat personal wi' dead Joseph Smith or God or whoever—they get the word straight from the horse's mouth, so t' speak, that the rules 'as been changed an' now they c'n only have one wife apiece. For bran' new religious reasons, y' see. Nothing t' do wi' the Supreme Court.'' He cackled. ''They all swear that's so. It ain't political, purely religious. Anyhow, the rules is changed right in th' middle o' the game, and now all o' a sudden this multiple wives stuff is old hat. They write it inta law an' everything. An' they're allowed t' become a state.

''Except there's still this old line bunch 'at wants t' keep on having things th' way they used t' be. Many wives as they please. So some o' them, they go kinda underground, like. Leave the newfangled one-wife crowd out in th' open, in th' big cities an' all, an' these old liners, they draw back inta the hills an' keep on marrying up wi' as many as they please.''

''I thought all that stuff was over a long time ago,'' Raider said.

''Aye. T' hear 'em tell it, it is. Except o' course it really ain't. An' that's where th' difference 'tween the saints an' the angels come in. The saints is the party line modern Moor-mons, see. Do what they're told an'

have one wife at a time. The crowd that won't let
themselfs be changed, they're th' angels. An' some of
'em take it a step further, see, an' think they're avengin'
angels. Doin' the will o' God. Or Joe Smith. Whichever 'tis they pray to. I never ha' got that straight, bein'
Catholic m'self an' doing what prayin' I do t' Jesus an'
Mary.''

Raider blinked. Jesus and Mary. Back there in that
cabin—no, it was on the path when Waters was killed—
the other ambusher had called out Jesus and Joseph.
Raider hadn't thought anything about it at the time.
Maybe he should have.

''So anyhow, there's these two bunches o' 'em, an'
they can't much stand each other. Bitter, some of 'em.
An' now, son, I'm hearin' that the saints, which is what
we got here in Jasper, are sayin' you're one o' them
avenging angels. Except me, I know better, 'cause I
brought you up that bottle for us t' share. An' there
ain't no Moor-mon, saint nor angel neither one, gonna
take a swaller o' fine whiskey. Dead against it, both
bunches. So I, um, kinda wanted t' have a word wi'
you. Give ye a bit o' warnin', like. Be kinda a good
idear was you t' watch your backside. If ye know what
I mean.''

The old man winked at him, recorked the bottle and
set it carefully onto the dresser top. ''Except I've taken
up enough o' your time, son. I thank you fer the drink.
And fer listenin' to my rambles.''

''You've been a big help, Willem. Thanks.'' Raider
dug into his pocket and handed the old bellman another
of Roy Sigmond's twenties. ''If you find the time t' get
around to it, you might find us another jug we can
share one o' these times.''

Willem chuckled and hesitated not a moment. The
twenty disappeared into his pocket with a magician's
speed. ''Thankee, son.''

''Thank you, Willem.''

Raider closed and bolted the hotel room door behind

the old man and pulled the chair over beside the dresser so he could spread his Chicago message and code book out side by side.

He hoped—and frankly suspected too—that whatever information the wire contained might well be more illuminating now that he'd had that chat with Willem.

Saints and angels. And a Pinkerton operative who was damn sure neither saint nor angel mixed in with them.

The question, he realized, was where Violet Thorn fit into that picture.

CHAPTER FORTY-THREE

Raider was grim faced and in a vile humor when he stepped out onto the sidewalk.

There were things in this life that he really didn't much mind. Good company. Good whiskey. Bad women. He could get along with those just fine.

Hell, he didn't even mind being used.

That was what the Pinkerton Agency did, really, when you thought about it. They set themselves out to be used. For an appropriate fee, of course.

But to be misused. Now that was something else again. To be abused. That was even more so. And at this point Raider was pissed. He'd been lied to, shot at, used, misused, abused, and just plain fucked over. He'd had just about a bellyfull of it.

He marched down the street to the telegraph office and slammed inside it. The telegrapher gave him a sheepish look but was wise enough not to offer explanations or apologies. In fact, the man kept his mouth clamped tight shut.

"Get out," Raider snapped. "I'll use the key my own self."

Even then the man didn't speak. Which was probably the best possible thing to do. He bobbed his head and left.

Raider waited until the front door was firmly closed

and no one would be listening in to his transmission, then sat at the telegrapher's desk and opened the line to the Evanston operator.

FOLLOWING MESSAGE TO ROY SIGMOND AT SALT LAKE CITY COMMA GRAND SIMEON HOTEL COMMA ALSO FEED TO SIGMOND INDUSTRIES COMMA SILVER CANYON UTAH STOP MESSAGE FOLLOWS

FOUND VIOLET STOP MEET ME GLORY HOLE UTAH SOONEST STOP SIGNED RAIDER

He considered adding a little something more, but the operator in Evanston wouldn't like that. Besides, Raider suspected there were laws against it. So maybe he'd better save his nasty mood for the end of this thing.

He closed the wire and stomped out of the telegraph office, leaving the door standing open and the office empty.

The Jasper telegrapher and a handful of friends were standing on the sidewalk at the end of the block, watching apprehensively as the tall Pinkerton operative turned and stormed away without a word or a backward glance.

CHAPTER FORTY-FOUR

"Hail, hail, the gang's all here," Raider muttered to himself. He was seated on a rickety chair in the shade in front of the Emil Lewis General Merchandise and Mining Supplies outfit in Glory Hole. Emil himself was mounted on his usual three-legged stool nearby. Raider had become well acquainted with the man over the past couple of days. Nice fellow.

Raider sat and watched the approach of a handsome brougham, it's canvas top erected against the sun. He couldn't see the occupants yet, but it was no trick to guess who they might be. Who else would be driving a rig fit for Paris in country like this? And with a pair of mounted outriders to guard them.

Raider could see and certainly recognize the guard on the left. That one was weasel quick and street smart little Ira Caldwell, derby hat, wire spectacles and all. Roy Sigmond's errand boy and half tame cobra.

The other outrider he hadn't seen before, but he recognized the type. A pistol with a price tag dangling from its trigger guard, all decked out in shirt and pants just like it was human. Yeah. Raider certainly recognized the type.

"Emil, my friend," he said softly, "I think it'd be nice if you was t' step inside an' brew us up a pot o' coffee or somethin'."

179

Lewis started to protest. He knew—but then Raider
did too—that there was still half a pot left over from
lunch. Then he looked up and saw the fancy brougham
coming down the road from the summit. Emil Lewis
coughed delicately into his fist, stood, and made his
way heavily inside the store building.

Raider didn't move. He sat with his chair tipped back
against the wall of the store and his coattails open.

The brougham drew nearer, and Ira Caldwell broke
away from it at a lope. He held the speed unnecessarily
close and dragged his horse to a sliding stop not three
feet from Raider's chair. Showing off. Showing this
handsome Pinkerton that while he might wear a derby
and play in the streets, Ira knew how to ride a horse.
Or by implication do anything else that Raider could
do as well.

The antagonism Raider'd felt since the first moment
he laid eyes on Ira Caldwell was still there, and in
spades, but he didn't let it show. Hell, he didn't have
to. Caldwell would be able to feel it every bit as
strongly as Raider did.

"I see the pup," Raider said dryly. "Where's the
master?"

Caldwell's eyes narrowed. He spun his horse as if to
head back up toward the oncoming brougham. The
horse's broad butt shifted close to Raider's chair when it
turned.

Raider lifted a boot toe, not hard but precisely placed,
into the tender crotch where the gelding's balls used to
be.

The gelding boogered into a squat-and-git, bolting
away from that boot and that chair just as quickly as it
could, and for a couple of seconds there Ira Caldwell was
hanging on with both hands and no doubt wanting to
holler whoa. His pride prevented that, and he somehow
managed to stay in the saddle. Caldwell raced—didn't
have much choice about that considering the speed the
gelding was traveling now—back up to the side of the

brougham and rode beside it at a much more sedate and controlled pace back to where Raider still patiently waited.

The low-slung door of the brougham opened, and Roy Sigmond stepped out.

There wasn't any sign of Sigmond's fancy filly of a wife Eleanor. Pity. Raider liked looking at her. She would've made the afternoon more enjoyable. But hell, he expected to enjoy it anyhow. He could live with the disappointment.

"Sigmond." He nodded.

"*Mister* Sigmond to you," Caldwell corrected. Ira wasn't taking any more chances on a horse ruffling his feathers. He dismounted quickly and practically jumped to attention at Roy Sigmond's side.

The brougham driver saw his passenger deposited safely on the ground and drove off in search of water for the team of handsomely matched blacks. The second guard dismounted and wandered in the vicinity with an eye on the surroundings so no one could sneak up on the boss. Raider knew there wasn't anyone else in Glory Hole who gave a shit about Roy Sigmond. But the guards wouldn't be sure about that, and he couldn't blame them.

"I was delighted with your wire, Mr. Raider. Truly delighted." Sigmond was so delighted he was practically wringing his hands with eagerness. "You will tell me where I can find dear Violet now, please?"

"You bet," Raider told him. "But first I wanta tell you a little story."

Caldwell started to say something snippy, but Sigmond cut the little man off with a wave of his hand. He was frowning now, though. "Mr. Raider, if you are trying to hold me up for an additional payment—"

"Pinkertons don't play that way, Sigmond."

"Yes. Of course. Sorry. But really, sir, I am most anxious to find Violet and—"

"Sit down. That stool there should do you. Hear me out." Raider smiled. "Humor me, okay?"

"Yes, um, if you wish."

Sigmond perched on the edge of the stool Emil Lewis had vacated.

"What this little tale is about, Sigmond, is lies. An' lies inside o' lies. Lies runnin' in all kinds o' circles."

"Mr. Raider. Please. I am most anxious—"

"Yeah, I know. I know you are." Raider smiled at Sigmond again. But his attention was on Ira Caldwell.

"I found Violet, Roy. She's half a day's ride from here."

"Good. Wonderful. I—"

"But I found out a couple other things too, Roy. Some I finally figured out for myself. Some the home office back in Chicago figured out for me. An' some Violet told me herself."

He expected a reaction to that one. He got it. Roy Sigmond clouded up like he was fixing to rain all over the Uinta Mountains. He sat up straighter and started to explain.

"Save it. Right now I'll talk; you'll listen. Right, Roy?"

Sigmond didn't like that worth a damn, but he held it in and kept his jaw closed. He fidgeted on Emil's stool, but he didn't jump or roar. The man had better control than Raider'd expected. Probably working up his next lie. Raider almost hoped he got to hear it. He always admired a truly inventive liar. It was an art not everybody could manage.

"Gettin' back t' my story, Sigmond, we gotta look at a few facts. For instance, y'see, the facts 'bout your dear sister Violet.

"Now ain't it funny how your ol' daddy died fourteen years ago? And how you had this brother who dropped dead not too long ago? And how this brother had hisself a wife. A fifth wife, actually. An' all of 'em at the same time. An' how this fifth an' youngest wife was his favorite. An' how this favorite was the one he willed all his shares in Sigmond Industries to."

Roy was really pissed by now. Raider kept talking.

"An' how there's this rule or custom or convenient revelation about how a brother's s'posed t' marry his dead brother's widows if one o' you asshole angel types shucks off this here mortal coil—which by the way, Roy, I'm kinda curious; did you marry the other four widows too? Or is sweet Violet a special case 'cause she holds legal right t' all them stock shares that'll make you even richer if you get your hands on 'em?

"An' how this here partic'lar widow name o' Violet 'd rather be a saint than a angel an' this time she'd ruther marry a man she loves 'stead o' one she's told t' marry, 'specially since she'd ruther be a one an' only wife 'stead o' one amongst a herd of 'em.

"An' how there's this feudin' an' fussin' amongst the saints an' the angels anyhow, so it don't take much t' get both sides worked up into what shoulda been a private affair.

"An' how there's this asshole son of a bitch name o' Sigmond that's tryin' t' force his brother's widow t' marry 'im so's he'll get control o' her stock certificates, 'bout which she don't give a shit nohow an' would've signed over if this asshole son of a bitch would've just asked polite, 'stead o' siccing th' asshole son of a bitch avenging fucking angels on her.

"An' how this asshole son of a bitch cain't do no good amongst the saints hisself 'cause him an' them are on the outs, so he tried t' hire it done inside a screen o' lies an' deceptions.

"Now do I have that right, Roy? Have I got any of it wrong? D'you wanna correct me 'bout it?"

Raider's tight, grim smile was directed toward Roy Sigmond, but his attention remained firmly fixed on Ira Caldwell.

"You son of a bitch," Sigmond said.

"Comin' from you, Roy, I'm proud t' hear that opinion. Anythin' else'd be an insult."

"I can pay you to—"

"You cain't pay me t' do a damn thing, Sigmond. There ain't that much money. An' you cain't get Violet back from Lester neither. Not with me. Not without me. What I suggest you can do, Sigmond, is go pack silver ore up your ass. Which is 'bout all the pleasure you're gonna get outta it. You know why? No? Well you don't have t' beg me t' tell you. I'll be proud to. 'Specially since I'm happy t' tell you it was my suggestion. Those stock certificates? They're on file in Salt Lake, y'know. An' Violet an' Lester happen t' have friends there.

"An' Lester—he's a pretty good fella, even if he does think he's a saint, which I personal think is pushin' it—but anyhow, him an' Violet, they don't want no part o' tryin' t' run a mine in angel country. So what they're gonna do, Roy, they're gonna sign those stock shares over t' the church. You know th' one. All full o' chest-thumpin' saints an' apostles an' whatever else you folks call 'em. An' these here latter day saints are gonna come in with the law an' whatever else it takes, an' they're gonna take over the majority ownership in them mines, Roy. They're gonna take right over an' run things up there in Silver Canyon however they please."

Raider laughed.

"Yeah, Roy, I can see from the look on you just how happy you are 'bout that."

Sigmond stood. He faced away from Raider, hands clasped behind his back. Raider didn't have to see the man's expression. The back of his neck was a bright, angry red.

"Kill him." Sigmond started down toward the trough where the driver was watering the brougham team.

"Kinda pissed, ain't he?" Raider said cheerfully.

"Kinda," Ira Caldwell agreed.

"You take your job serious enough t' die for it, Ira? Or d'you want t' walk away nice an' quiet so you'll be alive t'night when ol' Roy gets drunk an' hasta have his head held over a bucket?"

"I take my job seriously enough, mister. But even if I didn't, I'd do you just for the pleasure of it."

"Don't get along real extra well, do we, Ira?"

"You could say that, Raider."

"*Mister* Raider t' you, asshole."

"Any time you're ready."

Raider grinned at him.

Caldwell went through an act like a damn bullfighter primping up his suit of lights. He took off his coat and hiked up his sleeve garters and made strange faces and shot his jaw and flexed his fingers and strutted and pranced like a banty rooster in the hen fucking season. Raider thought the whole performance was funny as hell, really.

"Ready?" Caldwell demanded.

Raider grinned at the man again. He was still seated on the chair with the back tipped back against the wall of the store. He had his thumbs hooked behind the buckle of his gunbelt. He was loose and relaxed. Ira Caldwell looked like a clock spring wound up to the breaking point.

"Are you going to die standing on your feet, *Mister* Raider?"

"Hell, I dunno. Ask me in forty or fifty years, Ira."

Caldwell's hand swept into motion without any more posing or pretense. The bespectacled little man was quick and he was deadly.

He wasn't half quick enough. And he was no longer deadly.

Raider shot him in the stomach, in the chest, and then, carefully, in the head, the muzzle of the big Remington riding up with the recoil for each succeeding shot.

Ira Caldwell ceased to be a danger.

Down the way along the narrow road toward Jasper, Roy Sigmond's other guard stared in shocked surprise. And then turned and acted like he had seen nothing. Nothing at all.

Roy Sigmond, too, pretended nothing at all had happened. After a moment Sigmond climbed back into the brougham. The guard mounted his horse and took up a protective position to the left of Sigmond's rig. The driver shook his lines over the team, and the spanking rig rolled down the road and out of sight.

"Coffee's ready," Emil Lewis called from inside the store.

"Thank you, friend."

Raider figured he just about had time for a cup before he started back down toward Jasper.

There was a girl working at a haberdasher's there who would be getting off about seven o'clock. If he started soon and pushed the dun just a little, he figured he would hit town just about right.

Raider stood and went inside. He still had quite a lot of Roy Sigmond's expense money in his pocket. And he sure as hell didn't want to hang onto it long. Some of it, he figured, could go toward Ira Caldwell's burying. And that little gal at the haberdashery could benefit from the fun of some.

The only pity was that Sigmond wouldn't be needing burying. Raider grunted. A man couldn't expect to have everything.

He smiled at his friend Emil and accepted a steaming cup of strong coffee from the man.

"T' your good health, Emil."

"And to yours, Raider."

The hard-hitting, gun-slinging Pride of the
Pinkertons rides solo in this action-packed series.

J.D. HARDIN'S

RAIDER

Sharpshooting Pinkertons Doc and Raider are legends
in their own time, taking care of outlaws that the
local sheriffs can't handle. Doc has decided to settle
down and now Raider takes on the nastiest vermin
the Old West has to offer single-handedly...charming
the ladies along the way.

___BAJA DIABLO	0-425-11057-5/$2.95
___STAGECOACH RANSOM	0-425-11105-9/$2.95
___RIVERBOAT GOLD	0-425-11195-4/$2.95
___SINS OF THE GUNSLINGER	0-425-11315-9/$2.95
___WILDERNESS MANHUNT	0-425-11266-7/$2.95
___BLACK HILLS TRACKDOWN	0-425-11399-X/$2.95
___GUNFIGHTER'S SHOWDOWN	0-425-11461-9/$2.95
___THE ANDERSON VALLEY SHOOT-OUT	0-425-11542-9/$2.95
___THE YELLOWSTONE THIEVES	0-425-11619-0/$2.95
___THE ARKANSAS HELLRIDER	0-425-11650-6/$2.95
___BORDER WAR	0-425-11694-8/$2.95

Check book(s). Fill out coupon. Send to:

BERKLEY PUBLISHING GROUP
390 Murray Hill Pkwy., Dept. B
East Rutherford, NJ 07073

NAME_____

ADDRESS_____

CITY_____

STATE_____ZIP_____

PLEASE ALLOW 6 WEEKS FOR DELIVERY.
PRICES ARE SUBJECT TO CHANGE
WITHOUT NOTICE.

POSTAGE AND HANDLING:
$1.00 for one book, 25¢ for each ad-
ditional. Do not exceed $3.50.

BOOK TOTAL $_____

POSTAGE & HANDLING $_____

APPLICABLE SALES TAX $_____
(CA, NJ, NY, PA)

TOTAL AMOUNT DUE $_____

PAYABLE IN US FUNDS.
(No cash orders accepted.)

208

**A brand new Texas family saga
for fans of Louis L'Amour's Sacketts!**

BAD NEWS

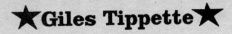

★Giles Tippette★

Justa Williams, a bold young Texan, has a
golden future ahead of him on his family's
ranch—until he finds himself trapped in the
tough town of Bandera, wrongly accused of
murder.

But Bandera's townfolk don't know Justa's
two brothers. One's as smart as the other is
wild—and they're gonna tear the town apart
to get at whoever set up their kin!

Look for more adventures featuring the hard-
fighting Williams family—coming soon!

_BAD NEWS   0-515-10104-4/$3.95

Check book(s). Fill out coupon. Send to:

BERKLEY PUBLISHING GROUP
390 Murray Hill Pkwy., Dept. B
East Rutherford, NJ 07073

NAME_____

ADDRESS_____

CITY_____

STATE_____ZIP_____

PLEASE ALLOW 6 WEEKS FOR DELIVERY.
PRICES ARE SUBJECT TO CHANGE
WITHOUT NOTICE.

POSTAGE AND HANDLING:
$1.00 for one book, 25¢ for each ad-
ditional. Do not exceed $3.50.

BOOK TOTAL	$____
POSTAGE & HANDLING	$____
APPLICABLE SALES TAX (CA, NJ, NY, PA)	$____
TOTAL AMOUNT DUE	$____

PAYABLE IN US FUNDS.
(No cash orders accepted.)

204